S0-CJY-067

THE LOST LIBRARY

Also by

Rebecca Stead and Wendy Mass

BOB

THE LOST LIBRARY

REBECCA STEAD

WENDY MASS

Feiwel and Friends
New York

A Feiwel and Friends Book
An imprint of Macmillan Publishing Group, LLC
120 Broadway, New York, NY 10271 • mackids.com

Library of Congress Cataloging-in-Publication Data
Names: Stead, Rebecca, author. | Mass, Wendy, 1967– author.
Title: The lost library / Rebecca Stead and Wendy Mass.
Description: First edition. | New York : Feiwel and Friends, 2023. |
Audience: Ages 8–12. | Audience: Grades 4–6. | Summary: When a
mysterious Little Free Library guarded by a large orange cat appears
overnight, eleven-year-old Evan plucks two weathered books from
its shelves, never suspecting that his life is about to change.
Identifiers: LCCN 2023018567 | ISBN 9781250838810 (hardcover)
Subjects: CYAC: Little free libraries—Fiction. | Books and reading—
Fiction. | Cats—Fiction. | Fantasy. | LCGFT: Fantasy fiction. | Novels.
Classification: LCC PZ7.S80857 Lo 2023 | DDC [Fic]—dc23
LC record available at https://lccn.loc.gov/2023018567

First edition, 2023
Book design by L. Whitt
Feiwel and Friends logo designed by Filomena Tuosto
Printed in the United States of America by Lakeside Book Company,
Harrisonburg, Virginia

ISBN 978-1-250-83881-0 (hardcover)
5 7 9 10 8 6 4

FOR THE LIBRARIANS OF THE
PAST, PRESENT, AND FUTURE

Chapter One
MORTIMER

Mortimer waited on the cool stone basement floor in front of mouse door number four, his fluffy orange body covering as much territory as it could. His paws were spread in front of him, as if he were about to catch a watermelon.

Books, in Mortimer's opinion, got it wrong about cats. In books, cats were usually stuck-up, sometimes even uncaring. As if cats had no feelings at all.

Cats had hearts, too.

Feelings, his heart said.

Mortimer had a lot of feelings. What he didn't have were a lot of words.

Mice were better with words than he was. Mice talked a *lot.*

The bell on top of Martinville Town Hall began to ring, as it did at 6:00 P.M. every day. The scratching behind the door was getting louder. A mouse would be coming through any second now.

"Apples!" he heard a small voice say. "I smell apples!" And behind the voice there were murmurs of excitement.

Here they come, Mortimer thought. He put on what he hoped was a gentle smile just as the first of the mice emerged, shaking off little bits of dirt and sawdust and, as usual, *talking.*

"Is that a . . . cat?"

A second mouse appeared. "What sort of terrible place is this, with a heartless *cat* standing by the door? This must be a bad dream!"

A third mouse popped through the hole. Mice, Mortimer knew, rarely traveled alone.

"Welcome!" Mortimer said. He glanced nervously at the potato bin. Last week, a mouse had managed to jump into it. Mortimer had had to wait for him, remaining perfectly still under the stairs, for almost three hours.

"Please follow me, mice." Mortimer tried to sound cheerful. "This way to outside!"

"But we just got *inside*!" one of them whined.

Using his outstretched arms like windshield wipers, Mortimer herded them to a small mouse hole in another corner of the basement (also known as mouse door number three). Mice, he'd learned, never liked to go out the same way they had come in.

"That horrible cat has six-toed feet! How terrifying!"

"Wait a minute. Could this cat be the Six-Toed Grouch?"

The exit, which was not far from the old library book cart, led outdoors, away from Ms. Scoggin, the apples, and Mr. Brock's cheese. And the potato bin.

"And now I suppose we are expected to go straight out into the cold again?"

In fact, seeing Mortimer and his sizable paws, the three of them were already crowding around the mouse hole, trying to leave.

"Not cold," Mortimer said. "It's summertime. Be careful, though—there's a road on the other side of this door. Cars. But everything is fine!"

"Oh, great," one of them said. "Thanks for nothing, Six-Toed Grouch." And he disappeared through the hole.

"And by the way, everything is NOT fine," the last mouse added. "I'm VERY hungry." But, keeping her eyes on Mortimer's paws (he actually did have six toes on each), the mouse squeezed herself through the hole, backward.

"Sorry," Mortimer said. "Keep moving, please. Sorry!"

"Cats are never sorry," said the mouse, just before vanishing into the night. "*Everyone* knows that cats have no feelings."

Mortimer didn't say anything. There was no point, because they were gone. He pressed his eye to the small hole, looking to see that they had made it safely across the road. "Goodbye," he whispered. "Goodbye and good luck."

Ms. Scoggin did not tolerate mice. By now, Mortimer knew that he couldn't stop them from coming in through the mouse holes (he'd carefully numbered them, mouse doors one through five). The mice had been coming for all the years he'd lived in the house, and there wasn't much he could do about it, other than gently guide them back outside again. He'd learned to hear their scritching and scratching and was always ready to meet them at a door and point them to the nearest exit.

Mortimer did not think of himself as good with words, but his hearing was excellent.

He tried to straighten up the basement. As usual, rushing around the way they did, the mice had banged into things.

Tonight, three apples had fallen from a tall wobbly shelf. Even with twenty-four toes, Mortimer could not pick up apples. But he could roll them to a spot near the stairs, where Al would be sure to see them right away. He lined them up for her.

Maybe they were not too bruised. Or she could make applesauce. Again.

When the basement was neat and quiet, he took a deep breath, savoring the smell of apple muffins that floated down the kitchen stairs. Al was baking, as she did most Sundays. Through one of the small, high basement windows, he saw the day's light fading. He exhaled, and felt happy.

Then his eye fell upon the cart of old library books. His happiness went quiet, and a guilty feeling wrapped around him like one of Al's hugs, which were always a little too tight.

My fault, his heart said, for the millionth time. *All my fault.*

He looked away.

Chapter Two

MORTIMER

Not long after the mice left, Al came downstairs. Ignoring the apples he'd lined up for her, she sat herself down on the basement floor, where she did not move for almost an hour.

She was staring at the library cart.

In twenty years, Al had never done that before.

Mortimer wondered if she needed a hug and went over to stand on one of her feet.

"Oh, dear cat!" she said, and reached for him.

Little too tight, Mortimer thought. But he allowed it.

When Al began to take the books off the cart, stacking them on the floor all around him, Mortimer closed his eyes.

That delicious book smell, his heart said.

He let himself think about the library and his kitten days.

Mortimer and his sister Petunia had loved their games. "Boss of the library" was Petunia's favorite. The rules were simple: Whoever climbed to the highest place was the winner. Mortimer, with his twenty-four toes, was a good climber, but he rarely won. Petunia climbed higher. She had six toes on every paw, just like he did. He could still remember her face, smiling down at him from the highest bookshelves in the old library stacks.

Once, she'd somehow made it up on top of the library's big blue doors! His eyes still closed, Mortimer remembered. Petunia was like a beautiful and triumphant snowball, way up near the ceiling. A *stuck* snowball.

Ms. Scoggin had stood on a chair to get her down.

Ms. Scoggin was Mortimer's favorite. Her hugs were never too tight.

These happy thoughts were interrupted by Al.

"Dear cat!" Al was clutching her notebook. He saw that she had drawn lot of *marks* on the library cart, and piled all the books onto it again. Messily.

Her cheeks were flushed. "We must wake Ms. Scoggin," she told him. "There is no time to lose."

He followed her upstairs and then right back down to the basement, now with Ms. Scoggin floating sleepily behind them. "I was having the most delightful dream," Ms. Scoggin told Al. "I dreamed I was at the movies! I believe it was the theater in Grantville. They have *superior* popcorn, my dear. You must go there. Please do."

Al shoved a plate of apple muffins at her and said, "I have a plan. And I need a lookout."

It was almost dawn when Mortimer realized that Al and Ms. Scoggin intended to push the library cart outside.

Outside! he told himself.

They are taking it away, his heart said.

This was a terrible idea, in Mortimer's opinion, and he told them so, until Ms. Scoggin pointed at him and said to Al, "Did you remember to feed the dear cat his dinner? He is meowing quite a bit!"

And Al said, "I did feed him. Maybe he's just feeling conversational." She leaned toward Mortimer and said, "Are you saying very important things, dear cat?"

How tiring, Mortimer thought. There must be another way. Because he did not want that library cart to go anywhere. And then, before he could make an actual plan, Al was pushing it toward the cellar door, and Ms. Scoggin was right behind her.

What should he do? This cart of old books was all that was left of his first home, his library. It was all that was left of his happy memories of kittenhood, and his Petunia.

All my fault, his heart said.

And now they were almost at the door.

He cried, "Stop!" and leapt from the floor to the top of the library cart.

But the cart kept moving. Mortimer's bulk was mostly fur. He only weighed about nine pounds.

Al laughed. "And away we go!"

Mortimer had never felt so misunderstood in his life. But he faced forward and stayed where he was.

My library! his heart said.

What is left of it, he reminded himself.

Outside, in the dark, Mortimer watched Al kneel in the grass and dismantle the library cart.

His library was in pieces. He had not been able to protect it after all.

Al sawed. She hammered. She glued.

Mortimer was getting a stomachache.

Then she pointed at a towel-wrapped bundle a few steps away. "Guess what's in there?" she asked Mortimer.

"Do not break the books," he told her. "Please do not hurt any books."

"Meow to you, too!" Al said, pulling the towel bundle toward them.

He looked at her. It did annoy him sometimes, the way she assumed he had no idea what she was saying, when in fact *she* was the one who could not understand *him*.

"Doors!" she said, lifting a small square of wood and glass out of the towel bundle.

The thing in her hands looked very familiar. Then he realized: It belonged to the little cabinet over the sink at home. The cheese cupboard doors! She had taken them both off their hinges!

Correction: She had taken the hinges, too.

And now, from one of her dress pockets, she produced a screwdriver.

He went to sit with Ms. Scoggin. "Oh good," she said. "You can help me be lookout. Meow twice if you see anyone coming."

Mortimer sighed. He hoped they could go home soon.

There was just a bit of light growing in the sky when Al finished her little-library-with-stolen-cheese-cupboard-doors.

Mortimer was tired. He trailed home after Ms. Scoggin and Al. But when he reached their porch, Mortimer realized that he could not go inside.

Not with my library outside, his heart said.

What is left of it, he reminded himself.

Mortimer turned around. He walked down the steps and away.

My library, his heart said, *still needs me.*

Chapter Three
EVAN

On the absolute last Monday morning of fifth grade, Evan climbed the dirt road that led from his house to the Martinville town green, where his school was.

"Climbed," because it was mostly one long hill.

Chapter Four
AL

Hold on, now. (I would say "take my hand," but we both know that this is impossible.)

The eye of the story has moved—the eye has left Mortimer the six-toed cat, and now it's looking at Evan the fifth grader.

Some people really dislike that.

But Evan and Mortimer live in the same town. In fact, they are about to cross paths. Briefly.

I live in Martinville, too. That's where all of this is happening.

It will make sense. Soon.

Chapter Five
EVAN AGAIN

Just ahead, Evan saw the magnolia tree that meant he was three quarters of the way to school. He checked his watch. By running a little bit, he had earned himself five free minutes. Evan loved making free time and then spending it however he wanted.

His back against the tree trunk, he looked down the hill he had just climbed. It was the "less fancy" part of Martinville: dirt road, no sidewalks or streetlights. To Evan, it was the most beautiful part of town: lots of trees and sky, and now that it was almost summer, everything was covered in a bright new green. (In the spring, Evan's road was usually muddy, and he loved it slightly less.)

He took two apples and his journal out of his backpack.

The apples were not "store apples." They didn't really get shiny, no matter how much he rubbed them. They were from the apple trees planted behind their house by his father's great-grandmother, or someone like that. The unshiny apples were lumpy shaped and kind of small, which was why Evan had two of them.

Sometimes in the cafeteria, kids said "ew" to Evan's apples, which was why he liked to eat them before school. They tasted perfectly great.

Evan found his pen, opened to a new journal page, and waited for an idea to bubble up. Mr. O'Neal said they could write about anything at all. But they were supposed to write *something* every day.

He waited. But no ideas bubbled up.

Instead, he thought about how, early that same morning, Mr. Vanderbilt, who was some kind of businessman, had shown up on Evan's front porch before breakfast, demanding a refund from his dad.

"What did you do, send them away for a long weekend?" he'd called through the screen door between the porch and the kitchen. "You were supposed to kill them!"

The mice in his house had come back just three days after Evan's dad had supposedly "exterminated" them, and now, Mr. Vanderbilt said, he was going to have to hire a "real exterminator" to do the job.

"Refund!" he shouted through the screen door.

Evan's father had sat down at the table and written Mr. Vanderbilt a check.

In fact, Evan knew that his dad did not kill any mice. He trapped them instead, in small cages, and then he drove them over the mountain, where he released them into some woods.

"I don't know why they can't stay put—it's a perfectly nice little forest," Evan's dad muttered after Mr. Vanderbilt left with his refund. "Plenty of berries and things."

"Too many owls?" Evan's mother guessed.

"Hmm," said his father. And he stomped down the cellar steps to his office.

His parents had had this conversation many times before.

A lot of people came for refunds.

Evan pressed his back against the tree trunk, swallowed the last of his apple, and watched the clouds traveling across the soft blue sky. They were the feathery kind. Evan's dad had taught him some things about clouds on their campouts.

He braced the journal on his bent knees and started writing: *Cirrus clouds are always high up, never low down. To me, they look like feathers, taste like hot chocolate, and smell like bug spray. Cirrus clouds can move really fast.*

He knew he couldn't smell the clouds. But they reminded him of camping out with his dad, sitting cross-legged on their sleeping bags and drinking hot chocolate for breakfast. There were always little bubbles of dry hot-chocolate powder floating on top, which Evan loved. When they finished their hot chocolate, they would make instant oatmeal in the same cups. And then his dad would say, "Let's go find a trail."

He didn't write all of that. Instead, he tossed both apple cores down the hill (not littering, his dad always said, because they would be eaten by grateful animals), stuffed his journal into his backpack, stood up, and put on his imaginary cape.

No one knew about the cape. His dad had "given" it to Evan way back in kindergarten, when Evan was having trouble saying goodbye at the classroom door in the mornings the way everyone was supposed to.

Evan had kept the imaginary cape all these years. In his mind, he knew exactly what it would look like, if it were real: a red felt triangle, with two strings to tie it on. Too small now, for sure. Evan was actually the tallest kid in his grade. And he really liked school. But he also liked his cape.

He checked his watch again, turned himself around, and marched toward school.

He was very close to town when he saw the little free library for the first time. It rose up ahead of him, little by little, as he climbed the last bit of hill. Evan didn't know right away that it *was* a library. All he saw was the back of it: a wooden rectangle, sitting on a pole. A new sign? Or maybe someone's art project?

As he got closer, he understood that he was looking at a box. He crossed the street, stepped onto the grassy town green, and walked all the way around it.

Aha.

It was not just a box on a pole. It was a box on a pole with a set of small glass doors on one side.

And behind the doors were books.

He was still early for school. No one else was near the strange book box, other than a large and beautiful orange cat, lying in the shade beneath it.

"I know you," Evan said. He *did* know this cat—Evan's mother called it Goldie. In the morning, Goldie was usually sitting in an upstairs window of Martinville's History House, about fifty steps away. Before this, Evan had never once seen the cat outside. But he was pretty sure it was the same cat.

"What are you doing out here?" Evan asked. The cat tipped his face up to the sun and blinked sleepily.

Evan turned his attention to the funny box of books.

When he pulled, the glass doors swung open easily. A smell floated out.

A smell like . . . *applesauce*? And . . . cheese? But mostly applesauce.

Strange. But it was a good smell.

A little handwritten sign was attached to the single shelf inside:

TAKE A BOOK, LEAVE A BOOK. OR BOTH.

Evan breathed in *applesauce (cheese?)* until there was no more room inside him for the air to go.

Take a book, leave a book. Or both.

Evan decided to take two books. The smallest two, which he figured was the same as taking one. He shoved them into his bag without looking at them, and then he carefully closed the glass doors. But that smell seemed to follow him all the way to school.

The cat stayed put.

Chapter Six

MORTIMER

Mortimer had slept for only a few hours, which was not enough sleep for a cat. He blinked at the boy, who was now opening the small library doors.

His library's first visitor! He summoned his strength and sat up.

The boy was Evan, he remembered. Like his hearing, Mortimer's memory was excellent. From his many hours of sitting at his upstairs window in the History House, Mortimer had learned a lot about the people of Martinville, including most of their names.

He watched the boy read Al's sign. TAKE A BOOK, LEAVE A BOOK. OR BOTH.

A face, Mortimer thought, *can also be a question mark.*

Unexpectedly, he felt his small heart pounding. He wanted this boy with a question-mark face to take a book.

Evan's hand darted into the library.

Good, Mortimer's heart said. *Good.*

As he watched Evan walk away, Mortimer felt his exhaustion return. But the sight of Al, who was now coming across the lawn with his food dish, gave him strength.

Chapter Seven
AL

I waited for the dear cat to come home.

He did not come.

Finally, I brought him his breakfast outside. We had both had a long night, and every long night should end with a good breakfast.

Chapter Eight
EVAN

There was only a week of fifth grade left, but Mr. O'Neal worked his students to the end. Everyone complained, but Evan loved Mr. O'Neal. He made up the best math games and never forced anyone to share their journal writing if they didn't want to.

When Evan thought about starting middle school next year, he sometimes got a little pain in his side. The summer was the only thing protecting him now.

"Did you see that box of books?" he asked Rafe first thing that morning. "On the green?"

Rafe was Evan's best friend. They'd been in the same class every year since kindergarten.

"It's called a little free library," Rafe said.

"Weird, right? Where did it come from?"

Rafe sighed. "I didn't get to see it up close."

Rafe was not allowed to cross Main Street by himself, which was why he hadn't seen the box of books—the *little free library*—up close. Evan's parents said, privately, that Rafe's parents were "overprotective," but Evan wasn't supposed to know that.

"It smells like applesauce when you open the doors," he told Rafe. "And Goldie was there."

"Who?"

"Goldie. The cat from the History House."

"You mean *Sunshine*. I'll check it out after school." Rafe was allowed to go to the town green after school, as long as he left before the crossing guard did. "Want to?"

"Can't," Evan said. "Math packet."

Their math packets were due on Tuesdays. Rafe didn't mention that he got his math packets done a lot faster than Evan did. Although that was definitely true.

After school, Evan dumped his books on the kitchen table, where he always did his homework. His mom walked in, talking into her telephone headset.

"Very good, Mr. Sloan. Now do you see the little green

dot? Click on *that*. No? Are you sure your arrow was *right on top* of the dot? Try just one more time? Ah! Success! I knew you would get the hang of it, Mr. Sloan. You're a natural."

Everyone said she was the most patient and encouraging tech-support person in Martinville. That was why she was usually on the phone. Evan's father had given her the headset for her last birthday.

She smiled at Evan and pointed to the fridge, meaning, "Have a snack."

He gave her a thumbs-up and opened his math notebook.

An hour and a half later, he was still at the table (now covered by his books, a glass half full of milk, two empty pudding cups, and a banana peel) when he heard his father kicking off his work boots on the porch.

"Hey, kiddo." His dad's smile, when it showed up, made Evan feel like everything was going to be great, no matter what. Soon he would go into his cellar office and stay there for hours, but he always sat down with Evan for a little while first. He pulled out a kitchen chair.

They told each other the news of the day. It wasn't a big-news day, but there was always *something* to say, if you thought about it. Evan told his dad about the little free library and reminded him that the fifth graders were going to visit Grantville Middle School that Wednesday. Evan's dad told him about finding a family of mice in someone's mailbox.

Evan had his journal open on the table, but his dad never tried to peek, which Evan appreciated.

"So where are these little free library books?" his dad asked, smiling again and looking around the table.

Evan lifted his math book to uncover them. They were *real* library books, he realized. Or they had been, once. They had those numbered stickers on the binding, like the books at school. But these were not from the library at school.

One was so skinny that it was barely a book. It was called *How to Write a Mystery Novel.*

The other one was a really beat-up book for little kids. A messy tape job made it impossible to even read the title. Evan hadn't noticed that when he'd grabbed it.

He glanced up at his father, whose face was, to Evan's surprise, bright red. First, his dad seemed frozen, but then he suddenly stood up, knocking over his chair and catching it right before it hit the floor.

"Dad?"

His father was already at the cellar door. "Lots of email to answer," he grunted. "See you at dinner."

Evan stared after him, listening to his big feet clomp down the steps. He reached for the taped-up book and opened it. Inside the mangled cover, there was a little pocket for the circulation card, just like inside the books at school. Except at the top of *this* card were the words *Martinville Library*.

That was weird. Because there *was* no Martinville Library. Not anymore. The Martinville Library, as everyone in town knew, had burned to the ground. Years and years ago.

He plucked the card out of its pocket. It was printed with columns for dates and names, one row for each time someone borrowed the book. The same name had been written there, again and again.

He flipped the card, checking front and back.

One name: *Edward McClelland*.

His *dad's* name.

He looked at the cellar door, which his father had left open a crack. The sound of keyboard clicking came up the stairs. Two more mouse complaints had come in, his mom had told him. No matter how far away his father drove them, a lot of those mice seemed to find their way home.

Chapter Nine
EVAN

Evan had an old-fashioned phone in his bedroom—the kind with a big round dial on the front. He and Rafe had bought a matching pair at a yard sale with their own money. They called them "the bat phones." Rafe wasn't allowed to have a cell phone because his parents were afraid he would catch "cell-phone addiction."

Evan had finally finished his math packet and collapsed on his bed with a chocolate chip granola bar when his bat phone started to ring.

"I checked out the little free library after school," Rafe said without a hello, "and I found this cool old book about growing tomatoes. I hope there's no tomato disease my parents will tell me I might catch."

Evan told Rafe everything: about finding his dad's name in one of the books he'd taken, and the way his dad had kind of run away after seeing it.

Correction: He told Rafe *almost* everything. He didn't mention that when he got up to his room, some impulse had made him shove both books deep under his bed. He felt like maybe he'd accidentally discovered something his dad was ashamed of?

"Whoa," Rafe said. "You mean, out of all the books in that box, you took your dad's favorite one? From when he was a kid? What are the chances of *that*?"

That was a good question, actually. What *were* the chances? Mr. O'Neal had just finished a week of math lessons about probability. In fact, it was the "probability" math packet that was due the next day. (On the last week of school, when the *other* fifth-grade class was building pyramids out of pretzels and marshmallows.)

"Do you think *all* those books are from the burned-down library?" Evan said.

"Mine is," Rafe said. "But there's only one way to find out."

And Evan said, "I'll meet you."

After they hung up, Evan ran through the kitchen, where his mom was chopping carrots and talking to another client on her headset. He mimed "going to town" by walking two fingers up his palm and pointing out the kitchen door. She gave him a thumbs-up and pointed to the carrots, which meant "be back for dinner."

Evan and Rafe didn't need to say where they would meet, because Rafe was only allowed as far as his own corner, and so Evan always met him there. Now Rafe stood there, calling out questions while Evan worked as quickly as he could at the little free library just across the street.

Luckily, it was close to dinnertime and no one else was around, aside from Goldie, who seemed to be trying to send Evan a message with his endless stare: *What do you think you are doing?*

"I'll put them back, I promise," Evan said. He had stacked all the books in piles on the grass and was sitting in the middle of them.

Rafe's notebook was open. "How many total?" he yelled.

"Forty-four books!" Evan called back.

"Did you count twice to confirm your data?"

"No! I can count to forty-four, Rafe!"

Rafe nodded reluctantly. "Okay. Start looking!"

Evan opened the top book on the closest stack, found the circulation card, and scanned it. "Library book!" he yelled. "No Dad!"

Rafe made a note.

In five minutes, Evan had checked every book. They were almost all marked *Martinville Library*. It took another two minutes to put the books back inside the little free library. When he had them nice and neat, the cat hopped up on top of it. It was a big jump.

"Hey, you're not as lazy as you look," Evan told him. "Who do you actually belong to?"

The cat settled himself, draping his paws possessively over the edge of the box so that they partly covered the glass doors.

"Okay, I'm going," Evan said. "You can have it back."

Rafe was still scribbling when Evan reached him. "Okay," Rafe said. "Out of forty-four books, forty of them are from the old Martinville Library."

Evan said, "People have probably already taken a bunch of them. And left a few."

"Agreed. And your dad's name was on ten cards."

"Ten out of forty?" Evan said. "You don't even need a pencil for that math."

"Better to be safe, though." Rafe shot him a smile and circled something with a flourish. "Your dad checked out exactly *one fourth* of the library books in there!"

"There's something else I noticed," Evan said.

"Yeah?"

"Every library book was returned on the same day."

"Seriously?"

"Yeah, there's a return date stamped on the cards, like they do at school. And the last date stamped on every card is November 5, 1999. It's weird, right?"

"That *is* weird. Maybe your dad knows why?"

"I doubt it. I mean, I guess he's read a lot of books, but he's not a librarian. And in 1999, he was"—Evan had to think for a second—"a teenager."

"He read a *lot* of books," Rafe said.

"Yeah, well, not anymore," Evan said. "I don't think he has time. He's always working."

Rafe nodded solemnly. "Saving the mice."

"He's not *saving* them—"

But Evan was cut off by a long, loud whistle, followed by two short ones. This was Rafe's call to come home, immediately.

Rafe closed his notebook, said, "Dinner!" and was gone.

It wasn't until after dinner that Evan realized there was still one more library book to check for his dad's name: *How to Write a Mystery Novel.* It was under his bed, with the taped-up one that his dad had read over and over. His cheek pressed to the floor, Evan fished it out and sat at his desk to open it.

The circulation card was there. Like all the others, the book had been returned on November 5, 1999. It had only been checked out once, and not by his father.

Evan reached for the phone.

"H. G. *Higgins*?" Rafe whispered. "*The* H. G. Higgins?"

"Yes! Can you believe it? In Martinville!"

"But it must be a joke," Rafe said.

"What do you mean?"

"You know, the book is *How to Write a Mystery Novel.* So, whoever borrowed it thought it would be funny to sign it out as *H. G. Higgins, famous mystery writer*. Get it?"

"Oh, yeah." Evan deflated instantly. "You're right. That was stupid of me—I guess I fell for it."

"*Not* stupid," Rafe said quickly. "You're in detective mode. So you have to be open to every possibility."

"Right." But Evan still felt a little bit dumb.

"How was dinner?" Rafe asked. "Was your dad still acting weird?"

Evan's dad had not been at dinner. His mom said he'd been called out to a job.

His dad *was* saving the mice. Evan knew that.

In bed that night, Evan looked again at the cover of *How to Write a Mystery Novel.* He'd had no idea there were books like this. Could a book really tell you how to write a book? No teacher had ever talked about that, not even Mr. O'Neal.

Lying back on his pillow, he opened it above his head and flinched. From somewhere within the pages, something had fallen lightly onto his chest. He plucked the something up.

It was a picture. Evan looked at it for a while and reached again for the bat phone.

"Rafe," Evan said, looking at the picture. "Why didn't they rebuild the library? After it burned down."

"It probably costs a whole lot of money to build a library. And maybe it was a respect thing?"

"Respect? I don't get it."

"Because, you know."

"I *don't* know. Spit it out."

"Because people died in the fire?"

Evan's heart gave a strange double thump.

"People died?"

Chapter Ten
AL

Well, yes. Sadly. People died.

This might be a good time to introduce myself.

I was the assistant librarian at the Martinville Library on the night it burned to the ground.

You can call me Al.

I live in Martinville's History House, not far from where the old library once stood. I moved in after the fire with my supervisor, Ms. Scoggin, and her patron, Mr. Brock. No one minds about the three of us living there—we hardly take up any room, being ghosts (plus cat).

Ms. Scoggin always says it was a very good thing we came, because we know how to take care of the house. I keep the dishes clean and neatly arranged in their wooden rack above the sink. I wash the windows and beat the rugs in the garden before dawn, when no one will catch sight of me (my invisibility skills are not impressive). I manage the potatoes and the apples in the cellar, making sure they have plenty of cool air so that they do not rot. And I cook: applesauce, potato pancakes, apple muffins, baked potatoes, apple dumplings, mashed potatoes, and, when I lack inspiration, more applesauce. (Ghosts don't eat very much, but they do eat.)

Mr. Brock does his part. He has been, for many years, our sweeper. Though mostly cloudlike, he's taught himself to grip our broom. The dear cat takes care of the mice. And Ms. Scoggin takes care of *us*, she says. By which she means: She encourages Mr. Brock's reading (as his librarian), she snuggles with the dear cat (because they both like that), and as my supervisor, she walks behind me, Reminding and Criticizing.

In the evenings, after I have cooked and washed up, we all relax together knowing that everything is in its right place.

Except, as Ms. Scoggin likes to say, for me.

Our house was once the home of the Martins, our town founders, and everything in it is kept *just as it was* when the family lived here a hundred and fifty years ago. We have no electricity, only candles and a fireplace. Our one toilet has a pull chain. The children always laugh at that. (There are public tours every Sunday and Tuesday, at noon.)

It really is a perfect house for ghosts.

Sometimes we hear children playing on the porch (from which there is a short path leading to the grassy town green). This morning, I peeked through the curtains and saw two small heads pressed together on the swing, emitting whispers and giggles. "I believe it's hide-and-seek again!" I told the others.

Ms. Scoggin and Mr. Brock pay absolutely no attention to the children or the tour groups. Last week, a class of third graders marched right through the parlor while the two of them just went on chatting, reading, and drinking their cups of tea, and there wasn't the slightest problem.

I, however, have always showed a distinct lack of talent for invisibility, which is why I always hide myself away on tour days during the hour between noon and one. (Most recently, I have been folding myself into the broom closet.) I do not wish to scare anyone, least of all a child. Over the years, I have found many excellent hiding spots in our house.

If *I* were ever invited to play hide-and-seek, I would certainly be the winner.

Of course, we didn't exactly plan to be housemates, Ms. Scoggin and myself. And I certainly *never* imagined I would find myself sharing a home with Mr. Brock, who paces around his bedroom turning the pages of his books. Every so often, he stops, throws open his door, and makes an announcement.

"Ms. Scoggin! This dog is heroic! This dog, Ms. Scoggin, what courage she has!"

Or, "Ms. Scoggin! They are almost to the mountain! At last! I can hardly wait to know what they will find there! What courage!"

Or, more soberly, "Ms. Scoggin, I do believe these three brothers are becoming the most extraordinary young men! What courage!"

Courage is Mr. Brock's favorite thing to discover in a book.

He addresses his announcements to Ms. Scoggin, never to me. He is always hoping, I believe, that I am not at home. I know how this sounds—unkind!—but Mr. Brock is only encouraging me to go out more.

My supervisor, Ms. Scoggin, also thinks I am too much

at home. There are so many important things to *do* in the world, she says.

But what, I ask her, can one small ghost like me do about the world?

And if I were *not* at home, who did Mr. Brock think would bring his plates of 4:00 P.M. cheese? Certainly not Ms. Scoggin. She has not taken herself into the kitchen for years. She prefers to supervise me from the parlor, where she claims the soft chair by the fireplace. Until his recent departure, the dear cat was usually near her (when he was not stationed at his window or patrolling the cellar for mice). Often, they shared her chair, which I brushed regularly. (Without electricity, a vacuum cleaner was useless). The dear cat is a comfort—to Ms. Scoggin, in particular. I do wish he would come home.

I am not a comfort. Ms. Scoggin often says that I am "a test," which I think we can agree is the *opposite* of a comfort.

Over the years, I have asked her many times why I must be a test. I never loved tests and do not wish to be one. Ms. Scoggin just rolls her eyes, exactly as she did in the old days, when I worked for her at the library. ("Take your place!" she used to shout at me as she prepared to open the beautiful blue library doors at 8:30 sharp in the mornings. And I'd scuttle behind the circulation desk. "Stand up straight!" she'd say. "Librarians do not slouch if they can help it!" And I would straighten my back.)

At first, her criticisms hurt my feelings, but then I understood that they were only part of Ms. Scoggin's gruffness. Perhaps this was what mothers were like, I imagined. I had come directly from the orphanage, so I was no expert about parental things.

Every morning, when I bring the day's first cup of tea to her bed and help her pin on her "Librarian" badge, Ms. Scoggin greets me the same way she used to in our library days: "Take your place, my dear!"

But if I ask her what better place there could be than this excellent house for three fine ghosts (and their cat), she just glares at me.

She calls me "my dear," because, deep down, she is fond of me, and also because ghosts have trouble remembering names. But in our library days, she always called me by my name, usually while pointing accusingly at a cart of books that needed to be reshelved, or perhaps waving a paper over her head while complaining that my handwriting was illegible.

Or to tell me that she had seen another mouse.

Or to let me know that the printer was out of paper.

Or that the balcony light bulbs appeared to be very dusty.

You get the idea.

In our cozy house, Ms. Scoggin is less concerned about dust. But when I venture down the path to run my Monday errands, she often calls after me from behind the front door. "Head high, my dear! Eyes up! Take your place in the world!"

I do try to lift up my eyes a little. But if I hear Mr. Brock's echoing "What courage!" I know that it has nothing to do with me.

Chapter Eleven
MORTIMER

Mortimer's window had shown him the moon on many nights, but it had not prepared him for his first night under the sky.

The sky!

The countless stars, his heart said, *and their light dust.*

The air!

Soft and warm, his heart said, *with wind tickles.*

The sounds!

The frogs' night singing. All at once, but also taking turns.

And how did they all know to stop singing at exactly the same moment?

That was pretty interesting.

* * *

Often, right after a thought played through his head, Mortimer heard a funny kind of echo. Ever since he was a kitten.

One night, not long before they were separated by the fire, Mortimer asked Petunia whether she had an echo, too. They were in the basement of the library, in their corner, ready to sleep.

"Silly," Petunia had said. "That is not an echo. An echo only repeats."

"What is it, then?"

"I think that's your heart talking."

"My *heart* talks?"

"In a way." And then Petunia rested one paw on Mortimer's neck and fell asleep.

He stretched out in the grass under his library, looked at the stars, thought of Petunia, and felt connected to the world.

And at the same time, a little lonely.

His upstairs window had shown him many things over the years. But now he could not help wondering what else his window had *not* shown him.

Suddenly, Mortimer heard voices. Loud voices. *Mouse* voices.

"Ya! Ya!" a small mouse voice said. "That's what I told him! *Ya!* Really loud! And then, I don't exactly know how, but I did it! I dropped it. And he was left holding it, wondering where I had gone!"

Laughter.

Mortimer scanned the grass until he saw three tiny figures moving in a line.

Dropped what, he wondered? And who was left holding it? But he knew that if he asked, they would all start yelling at him or running away. So he stayed very quiet.

"You showed him, Finn!" someone said. "*Take that, you dumb old owl!*"

"Actually, I think it was a hawk," Finn said.

"Oh. Take that, you dumb hawk!"

"I'm proud of you," another voice said. "And in a few weeks, you'll be good as new."

"Yes, Mama."

Mama? Mortimer twitched. A mama mouse. He had never really thought about it before, but of course mice had mothers. It made sense.

"Tell me the truth, honey. Did it hurt?"

"No, Mama."

They weren't walking toward the History House, so Mortimer tried not to worry about the five unguarded mouse doors.

He tried not to think about the apples, the potato bins, or Mr. Brock's now-doorless cheese cupboard.

He just listened, until he couldn't hear them anymore.

Mortimer could still remember his own mother, a little bit: She was soft. And fierce. Mostly gray, with white feet that made her look like she was wearing socks.

He looked at the stars and hoped that Petunia, wherever she was, could see them, too.

Chapter Twelve
EVAN

"It's called a *Polaroid* picture," Evan's mother told him at breakfast the next morning. "I haven't seen one in a long time. Polaroids were the first instant cameras. Load the film, push a button, and your picture pops out the front!" She smiled. "But this one's a little bit like the world's worst selfie, isn't it?"

"Yeah, it is," Evan said. It was.

The picture in her hand showed what looked like an accidental corner of someone's face—half an eye and a little bit of the someone's glasses. In the distance, a tiny town, surrounded by red and orange trees. It had been taken in the fall, from somewhere high up, as if the photographer had been standing on a hilltop. Or maybe through a window?

His mom held it at arm's length and squinted. "This could be Martinville, don't you think? I think that's town hall."

One of the buildings *did* look like their town hall. But it wasn't quite Martinville, Evan thought. Something was off.

"Too small to tell for sure," his mom said. "Where'd you find this?" She handed the picture back.

"It was in one of those little free library books."

"Really? How mysterious."

"Where do you think all those books came from?"

"Someone's attic, I'm guessing. Finish that milk."

Why, Evan wondered, downing his milk, would someone have an attic full of random library books that were returned by different people on the same day? He stuffed two bumpy apples into his lunch bag.

"Last Tuesday of fifth grade!" His mom flopped dramatically into a chair. "Boy, that went fast. It feels like I was picking you up from kindergarten only yesterday. You really loved that plastic castle in the kindergarten playground. You spent *hours* in there, remember? I'd have to lure you out with a cookie or something."

"I know, Mom." He bent to give her a quick goodbye hug. She'd been counting down to graduation for a month, and he wished she would stop. It made him think about next year: the school bus, and middle school in Grantville, with new teachers and all those kids he had never met. Everything he *didn't* want to think about.

He'd never say it to anyone, but sometimes Evan wanted time to slow down. Or maybe they could add a sixth grade to Martinville Elementary? And Mr. O'Neal could teach it. And he and Rafe would have desks right next to each other, even though in real life teachers always put them on opposite sides of the classroom.

None of that would happen. It was what his dad called wishful thinking. Evan let the screen door bang behind him. When his dad heard the door bang in the morning, he always called out from wherever he was (usually his office in the cellar, which had a small window onto the driveway): "See you later, kid!" or "Have a good one, Ev!"

Not today.

Evan broke into a run at the end of their driveway. By the time he reached his magnolia tree, he was sweating and had saved up seven minutes. He threw down his backpack, drank half the water in his water bottle, and reached for his journal. But he surprised himself by pulling out *How to Write a Mystery Novel* instead.

The night before, he had read the first three chapters: *Setting*, *Tone*, and *Protagonists*. These turned out to be pretty good "falling asleep" chapters. But Chapter Four was called

Antagonists, which sounded more interesting. (And *Clues* was Chapter Five.) Evan studied the circulation card again, and the only name on it: *H. G. Higgins*, written in big, curly letters.

Ten minutes later, he looked at his watch and jumped up—now he would have to run again. And he'd forgotten to eat his apples.

He was about to tie on his imaginary cape when an image rose up in his mind: a detective's cap, like the one Sherlock Holmes wore.

That cape really *was* too small.

Instead, he drew his thumbnail down the middle of his forehead, adjusting his (imagined) cap. The gesture felt strangely natural. Evan smiled. And began to run.

At his desk, Evan got comfortable, opened his journal, and ripped out a page as neatly as he could. He had decided, at the end of his sprint to school, to write a letter.

Dear H. G. Higgins,

You don't know me, but I'm reading a library book that you maybe read, a really long time ago. It's called *How to Write a Mystery Novel*. At least I think you read it—your name is in it. Did you ever go to the Martinville Library? It burned down before I was born, so I've never been there, even though I've lived in Martinville for my whole life. Did you use to live around here? I think if you lived here, I would know about it, because you're a famous writer and this town is pretty small. I haven't read any of your books yet, but I know that *Assignment Accepted* was made into a movie. Did you get to be in it?

Next year I'm starting sixth grade at Grantville Middle. This probably sounds weird, but did you ever take a Polaroid picture and put it in that book? Do you wear glasses? Your name is actually the only one on the circulation card.

Thank you, even though you probably don't remember.

Evan McClelland

P. S. If you lived here, you don't remember someone named Edward McClelland, do you?
P. P. S. The book says that an antagonist has to be an obstacle to the protagonist getting what he wants. Do you agree with that?

Mr. O'Neal kept an "author correspondence center" at the back of their classroom, stocked with envelopes, stamps, and a cardboard mailbox. (Mr. O'Neal took the letters to the real post office himself.) Evan addressed his envelope to *H. G. Higgins, mystery writer*, and copied the address he found for H. G. Higgins on the internet. It wasn't a real address—it was "care of" a publisher in New York. Maybe H. G. Higgins didn't want people knowing where he lived?

Rafe was probably right. It probably wasn't the *real* H. G. Higgins who borrowed *How to Write a Mystery Novel* from the Martinville Library almost twenty years ago. But, like Rafe also said, Evan was thinking like a detective. And a real detective tracked down every possible lead.

Even the great Mr. O'Neal couldn't keep his fifth graders calm on the third to last day of elementary school. There was a nonstop buzzing excitement about graduation on Friday and the big picnic afterward for the fifth graders and their families—it was finally *their turn. This was it.* There was always one more thing to say, to whoever happened to be standing next to you.

After recess, Mr. O'Neal lined them up and held up both hands for quiet, looking serious.

"When we get to the classroom," he said gently, "every one of us is going to sit down with a book, take two deep breaths, and then read for half an hour. You all need a break from talking. And I need a break from trying to get you to stop talking."

Everyone laughed. For a second, they thought they had been in trouble. And it was actually a relief, to open their books and let their mouths rest for a little while. Though the buzzing feeling didn't really go away.

Evan had been reading *How to Write a Mystery Novel* for ten minutes when he realized that Mr. O'Neal was looking over his shoulder.

"Interesting. Are you planning to write a book this summer?"

Evan tried to decide if Mr. O'Neal was teasing him, and decided (correctly) that he was not. "No. But I am—" Evan realized he was about to say *but I am kind of trying to solve a mystery.*

Mr. O'Neal looked at him.

"But I am thinking about some stuff," Evan said instead.

Mr. O'Neal nodded. "All of life is a mystery, in a way. And that makes every single one of us a detective." He continued down the row of desks.

Evan just sat there for a few seconds, looking at his desk. He *was* trying to solve a mystery, he realized: the mystery of the little free library, and why it was full of books from a library that burned down twenty years ago. The mystery of H. G. Higgins and the Polaroid picture.

The mystery of why his father had banged out of the kitchen like that.

He took out his journal and flipped to the first empty page.

My Mystery, he wrote at the top. He would do an outline, like his book said to. If an outline worked for *writing* a mystery, maybe it would help him solve one. He copied the sample in the book and started filling out his answers.

SETTING: That was obvious. He wrote Martinville.

TONE: Evan thought about it, but only for a few seconds, and wrote Not scary. He did not enjoy scary stories.

PROTAGONIST: The "protagonist," the book said, was the person the story followed—and usually that was also the person who solved the mystery. It could be an actual detective, or it could be an "amateur sleuth," who could be pretty much anyone—town baker, newspaper writer, school principal. Fifth grader?

Me, he wrote. Amateur sleuth and fifth grader. And he drew the back of his thumb down his forehead, adjusting his imaginary cap.

ANTAGONIST: "Antagonist" usually meant "bad guy." But sometimes it didn't. Something else could get in the protagonist's way, like a storm, or a demented bear. Evan was the protagonist, so he asked himself, *What's in* my *way*? And then he wrote his answer slowly, while a tiny chill traveled up his back: Secrets.

SUPPORTING CHARACTERS: He hadn't read that chapter yet, so he just wrote Rafe.

CRIME: This wasn't *that* kind of mystery, which was a good thing. He left it blank.

MOTIVE: Evan thought he knew what "motive" meant—wasn't it the hidden reason the bad guy did whatever he did? But that was a guess. He left it blank.

VICTIM: Blank.

SUSPECTS: Blank.

CLUES: Finally! Now he wrote quickly. Why did Dad get upset? Where did that funny library come from and why is it full of old Martinville Library books? Why were all the books returned the same day? Did H. G. Higgins really live in Martinville? Who took that Polaroid picture? Why was it in the book?

Evan sat back in his chair, disappointed. Were these really clues? Or were they just a bunch of questions?

That was as far as he got. Twenty-nine of Mr. O'Neal's "thirty minutes of peace and quiet" had passed in near silence, but now the voices were rising around him. Evan was relieved to join them.

Chapter Thirteen
AL

Tuesday, and the dear cat has not yet come home.

Ms. Scoggin says if I stop bringing him his dish, he'll be back soon enough, but I can't bear to disappoint him.

Today's Tuesday Tour was a lovely fourth-grade class. From my broom closet, I could hear them shuffling from room to room and giggling at our toilet. Mrs. Baker, our tour guide, did an excellent job, as usual. But, as you can imagine, I have heard the "Martinville History House Tour Speech" many, many times, and so I sometimes tune it out. Today, chin resting comfortably on knees, I closed my eyes and visited one of my happiest memories from my assistant librarian days: book club.

* * *

Before I was a ghost, my favorite thing was Wednesday Book Club.

On book club days, I was happy at work, even if Ms. Scoggin had given me five Reminders and seven Criticisms before lunchtime. At three o'clock, I pretended to dust the windowsills and watched my book club members arrive, in ones and twos. Through the big front windows, I saw them get distracted by the bakery window or the stationery store with its comic book rack just inside the front door. (I had several times asked Ms. Scoggin if we might have a comics section in our library, but this led only to more Reminders and Criticisms.)

Sadly, I can't remember their names anymore. There were seven or eight "regulars" every Wednesday. Plus the boy.

The boy always came to the library on Book Club Wednesdays, and on many other days as well. He walked the same path from the school to our library, but he wasn't like the others. I could see that he was mostly distracted by his own thoughts, and as I watched, I wondered what they were.

At first, he barely looked at me, even when he came to the checkout desk with his pile of books. Once, he showed up with a damaged return—and he had tried to repair the book himself, with tape. He walked in and brought the book straight to Ms. Scoggin, and when she held it up, I nearly leaped over my desk to shield the boy from the Criticisms that were about to rain down on him. His face was pointed at the floor, but I could see that his ears were already bright red. And she had not yet begun.

But she said nothing. She merely gathered up the broken book with the others and said, "All on time, thank you," before turning away. Released, the boy flashed her a look of—disbelief? gratitude?—and then zipped away into the cool of the library stacks. I stood in near shock—Ms. Scoggin, I sometimes forgot, was a very nice person! Despite her Reminders. And her Criticisms. I thought, again, of mothers. I had a sudden urge to dust the light bulbs on the balcony, just to make her happy.

At closing time, I found her hunched over the work table in the basement, carefully taping up the book's spine. "Anyone could see that the child did not damage this book," she said. "It was probably some brute bully. Why are you standing there with your mouth open? Don't you have things to do?"

I gathered myself and said, "I have just finished dusting the balcony, Ms. Scoggin."

She nodded. "I hope you didn't forget the light bulbs."

I assured her that I had not.

But I have gone off on a tangent about Ms. Scoggin! I was telling about Book Club Wednesdays. The club members were Great Readers, and we had a wonderful time listening to one another talk about the books we were reading, what the stories were and what we thought might happen next, and how all of it made us feel. These young readers felt things about books, which is why I call them Great Readers. Being a Great Reader has nothing to with reading great sophisticated books, or reading great *long* books, or even with reading a great *many* books.

Being a Great Reader means feeling something about books.

I had created a special book club area, with a small rug around which I pulled up several book carts on Wednesday afternoons, to make protective walls. It was our club room, and the door was always open. Actually, there was no door, only a space between two of the carts.

But the point is that anyone could join our club—the members even posted invitations, on the bulletin board near the big blue doors, and at the school, in the town hall waiting room, and even in the grocery store parking lot. "All Welcome," they said at the top.

Every Wednesday, I hoped the boy would join us on the rug, and every Wednesday he did not. Instead, he sat at one of the library's two long tables, always in the chair *closest* to the rug, but with his back to us. And he was usually in his place well before our meeting began, so that it seemed (almost) to be a coincidence he was there. Which I knew it was not.

You have probably heard that you are supposed to be quiet in a library, but this was not true on Book Club Wednesdays. We did not even try to keep our voices down, but Ms. Scoggin never said a word. If something funny was said (we liked to joke), I would sometimes glance over at the boy and see, from behind, just a hint of a rounded cheek, which meant he was smiling. But he never came to sit with us.

Recognizing his cheek smile one Wednesday, I impulsively called out his name and said, "Please come and join us!"

The boy seemed to shrink in his chair. He picked up his stack of books with both hands (it was always a stack, with him) and hurried away without looking back. I was very worried that he would not be there the following

Wednesday, but he was. I never called out to him like that again.

The book club rug was our safe place, a place where you could say what you thought. One day, after I shared a particular book, one that meant a lot to me, a club member spoke up to say that he had read it already and found it extremely boring. I listened to him, and he listened to me. And that was fine.

I am not upset when others don't love the books I love. We each have our own book spaces inside us, and they do not match up perfectly, nor should they. The club members said goodbye that day as usual, all of us feeling like good friends.

A few days later, the boy came into the library. It was Saturday, and he was there first thing in the morning, carrying his returns. But instead of going straight to the book-return chute as he usually did, he carried his pile to my desk. I assumed Ms. Scoggin's "brute bully" had ripped the cover off another one and prepared myself to reassure him. He placed the pile in front of me without a word, and I made my way through them, stamping each one with my date stamper. No ripped covers.

Then I saw that the last book in his pile was the very

one I had talked about at Wednesday Book Club that week, the one I especially loved.

"Oh!" I said, and looked up, expecting to see the top of the boy's head, because he generally looked only at the floor. But not this time. He was looking straight at me.

He covered the book with one hand, fingers spread, and announced, "*Not* boring."

And then, for absolutely no good reason, tears filled my eyes. I told myself not to blink.

For a few moments, we looked at each other, his hand still covering my book protectively.

And then he turned and hurried away.

From that day forward, the boy brought his returns to me from time to time. When he did, I knew there was a special book in his pile: a book that, for him, contained much. And I knew that when I got to it, he would simply cover it with his hand and meet my eye for a moment.

Not all Great Readers wish to be in a book club. There are other ways of sharing books, with very little conversation, or none at all.

Chapter Fourteen

MORTIMER

A few people had brought a book, or two, and squeezed them into his little library on its first day. One book had been left with a sticky note attached: *My 100% FAVORITE book of fifth grade!!!* That book had been taken by a fourth grader within minutes.

Mortimer felt content. More and more so, in fact.

The first *crate* of books arrived on the second day, Tuesday, right after lunch. (Al was still bringing Mortimer's meals to him. She also sneaked in a few tight hugs, but he didn't mind.)

The crate was carried by Mr. Gregorian, who managed the grocery store. First, he tried to cram his books into

Mortimer's little library, but when he saw that they would not all fit, Mr. Gregorian made a decision. He set his crate on the ground under the library.

Exactly in the spot where Mortimer had made his bed. He glared up at Mr. Gregorian.

Mr. Gregorian said, "I can tell that you approve, Buffy. Good girl!"

People, Mortimer thought.

"Nothing wrong with adding a room to your library, am I right?"

With this, Mortimer had to agree.

Mr. Gregorian, after considering, carefully tilted the crate onto one side. "This'll help keep the rain out," he explained.

It was an egg crate, Mortimer realized. From his History House window, he had enjoyed watching the farmers bring their deliveries. Eggs came to Mr. Gregorian's store twice a week.

Mortimer hopped up on top of the crate. It was acceptable.

Late that evening, he heard mouse voices again.

"I *definitely* smell cheese. I'm telling you, it's here *somewhere*."

There were only two of them this time, zigzagging across the grass in the moonlight. Silent, Mortimer watched them come closer and closer.

"You can't smell it? Now it's even stronger!"

He could see them pretty clearly now—they were the same size and color, but they weren't exactly a matched set. One of them had a short tail.

"Oh, *that* was it—your *tail*!" Mortimer erupted.

And the mice froze right in front of him.

Belatedly, Mortimer closed his mouth. Oops. Now they would probably run away or start calling him names. He waited to see which it would be.

But they did neither. Some instinct had paralyzed them. Or almost, because he could see both of them quivering. The mice had sounded so brave the night before. Maybe they were just acting brave?

Mortimer took a slow backward step to see if that would release them. "I'm not—" he started, "I mean, I won't *do* anything to you."

"Finn, it's just the Grouch!" one of them said. His tiny body had relaxed visibly, but Finn was still stiff as a board.

"Finn," the mouse said. "Shake it off. We're okay! The Grouch doesn't bite."

Finn was trying to shake it off. Mortimer could tell.

Still looking mostly frozen, Finn said, "Ha. Close one!" and smiled weakly.

Mortimer took another step back and spoke quietly. "It was your *tail* that you dropped, wasn't it? And the hawk was left holding it—your tail? You escaped?"

Finn nodded.

Mortimer glanced at his own tail. *Ouch,* he thought.

"It's different for us mice," Finn said quietly. "We're *built* to do it. It's like . . . an escape trick."

The other mouse nodded and glanced at where the tip of Finn's tail used to be. "Right in the *nick* of time," the mouse said. "It was very well done."

"And your tail will grow back?" Mortimer asked.

Again, Finn nodded. "That's what my mom says."

Interesting.

"Do either of you happen to know," Mortimer asked, because these mice seemed to know things, "why the frogs sing at night?"

Both mice shrugged.

"Then I guess you wouldn't know how they all know to *stop* singing, at the same time?"

The mice looked at each other. "Never thought about it," Finn mumbled.

"Is there cheese in that cupboard up there, by any

chance?" Finn's friend was pointing up at the library. "It sure *smells* like cheese."

The cheese cupboard doors, Mortimer realized, *still smell like cheese*. "I'm sorry," he said stiffly. "This is a library. No cheese around here."

The mouse shrugged. "Okay. We have to find food soon, so we should probably get going."

"Hungry," Finn added softly.

Mortimer watched them back slowly away, turn around, and run.

He almost wished he had told them where to find the potato bin.

But that would upset Ms. Scoggin.

It was confusing.

Chapter Fifteen
EVAN

Evan expected Wednesday's trip to Grantville Middle School to be more loud, happy talking and no one able to sit still. And it *had* been that way, on the bus ride *to* Grantville. Mr. O'Neal had wanted to play math games, but the other fifth-grade teacher blasted her playlist on a portable speaker instead. Everybody sang. By the time they pulled up in front of the massive "Go Tigers!" banner hanging over the school's front doors, Mr. O'Neal was singing, too.

But going home to Martinville, everything was different. Kids mostly whispered as they got back on the bus. No one laughed.

"It's weird, isn't it?" Rafe said, flipping through his deck of baseball cards as they pulled out onto the road. "We're never going back to our school after Friday. After Friday, *that's* our school."

Evan had always imagined Grantville Middle as a lot like Martinville Elementary, just farther away, with different teachers and more kids. But it wasn't like elementary school. The kids there were huge, for one thing.

They'd had an assembly, where some graduating eighth graders sat on the edge of the stage and answered questions from the incoming fifth graders. Those eighth graders were super nice. But the buzzer that rang between classes was so *loud*, and the halls were so crowded with huge kids and their huge backpacks. The cafeteria was chaos. Everything looked kind of grimy.

"I remember the day I was sitting where you are now," one eighth grader had told them, his legs dangling off the edge of the stage. He wasn't from Martinville, so Evan didn't know him. "And I thought it seemed really big and weird here. But I promise—Grantville will feel like your place pretty fast. Today I feel sad about leaving middle school, just like you probably feel sad about leaving your schools."

He was one of those kids who could say what he meant, without being embarrassed. Like Rafe. Evan sat in the second row and wished he were more like that. He stared at the kid's legs. They were so long. They were hairy! Would his legs be that hairy in three years? He didn't want to think about it. Next year, the middle school bus would pick up Evan right in front of his house. There would be no more walks up the road, for thinking and eating his apples.

Everyone around him suddenly groaned loudly. Evan had missed something.

He turned to Rafe. "What happened?"

"No recess in middle school," Rafe said. "No *recess*."

On the bus ride home, even Mr. O'Neal thought it was a little too quiet.

"How about a game of Geography?" he called out. So they started playing, row by row. "Arizona," "Alabama," "Arkansas," "Seattle . . ."

Evan stared out the window as the bus climbed a hill. Suddenly, Martinville appeared below them, with the town green and the three roads that led to it all neatly laid out. Their school, the town hall, the History House, the shops, and big houses near town. Evan felt that almost-pain zip up his middle again, as if he were being forced to leave home. His eye traveled from one building to the next while his heart hurt.

"See? Right there. That's where it was." Rafe pointed through the window with a baseball card.

"Where what was?"

"The Martinville Library!" Evan followed the line of the baseball card. Between the town hall and the History House, and set back behind them a little, there was a big patch of—nothing. Bushes and stuff. Overgrown weeds.

He leaned forward and tried to see some sign of the old library, but as the bus went down the other side of the hill, trees got in the way and the town blinked out of view.

"You always knew it was right there?" Evan said.

Rafe nodded. "Yep. But I never really thought about it, you know? My parents always told me not to go in there."

"They're always telling you not to go *anywhere*," Evan said, almost rudely.

"I know." Rafe sighed.

A voice floated back to them from two seats ahead—Mr. O'Neal's. "I still miss it dearly. It was such a fine old library," he said, "with a turret and a steeple. Big blue doors. A creaky old balcony. The most wonderful librarians."

"How did the fire start, Mr. O'Neal?" Rafe called back.

Around them, kids were still playing Geography. "Mississippi," "Illinois," "San Francisco . . ."

Mr. O'Neal turned around, looking surprised. "No one knows how it started."

Evan and Rafe exchanged looks. "Really?" Rafe said. "That's weird, isn't it? Maybe it was lightning."

"No. Not lightning." Mr. O'Neal hesitated, and seemed to be looking at Evan.

Looking at him pretty strangely, actually.

"The fire started in the basement," he said finally. "But no one knows how it happened. Not for sure. I mean, it was nobody's *fault*. I'm sure of that."

"How do you know for sure?" Rafe said.

"It was a wonderful place," Mr. O'Neal said, as if that answered the question. And then they were looking at the back of his head.

"You can't say 'Philly,'" someone behind them was arguing. "You have to use the real name. 'Philadelphia.' You're just trying to give me a *Y*! Nothing starts with *Y*."

And then kids started yelling out the names of places that start with *Y*, and the last-week-of-school buzz was back.

When the bus pulled into the school parking lot, Rafe's parents were both standing there waiting for it. He waved at them from the window, and his mom threw her arms around him as soon as his feet hit the ground. As if Rafe had been away for a week instead of an afternoon.

"Well?" Rafe's dad said.

And Rafe said, "It was good," and waved bye to Evan.

There was a little crowd of parents, actually. But Evan didn't even look for his. They had trusted him to get home on his own since the end of third grade.

But then he heard Rafe call out. "Hey, Ev—there's your dad!" And he pointed across the street.

His dad was standing at the edge of the town green, apart from all the other parents. He was under a tree, slightly bent, as if the space was a little too small for him.

"Dad!" Evan called. He watched his father find him in the crowd of kids and break into a smile. Evan jogged over. "I didn't know you'd be here. Hi."

His dad put one big hand on Evan's head. "I was in town and saw everyone waiting, so I figured your bus was coming. How was GMS? Are the walls still mint green? Does the gym still smell like floor polish?"

"Yes and yes. And the bells are so loud. The cafeteria is gross. I'm glad we didn't have to eat lunch there."

His dad laughed. "Stop. You're making me miss the special flavor of GMS frozen fish sticks! Believe it or not, they grow on you."

"Edward?" Mr. O'Neal was crossing to where they stood. "Do you have a minute?"

"Of course. Everything okay?"

"Oh, for sure," Mr. O'Neal said. "Everything is great. Just one tiny thing."

"Two seconds, Evan!" his dad said, and followed Mr. O'Neal to the water fountain, where Mr. O'Neal took a long drink, wiped his mouth, and spoke in a low voice. His dad just listened. And then Mr. O'Neal handed him something, which his dad slid into his back pocket.

"What was that?" Evan asked when he was back.

"Nothing to worry about, kiddo."

"Was it another mouse complaint?"

For some reason, his dad laughed at that. Evan didn't think the mouse complaints were funny. He didn't know his dad thought they were funny, either.

"Nope. Just some . . . um, paperwork."

"Oh."

Paperwork?

Chapter Sixteen
AL

The house feels different without the library cart in the basement. *We* are different. The dear cat remains outdoors with the books. And now suddenly Mr. Brock can't keep hold of the broom. It passes right through his fingers.

Another thing: Supper has become quite somber. Last night, Mr. Brock, after so many years of cheerful suppertime book chatter with Ms. Scoggin, just gazed at his potato or looked sadly at the book on his lap.

He sniffed loudly and said, "Ms. Scoggin, the young woman in this story is being treated most unfairly. *Most* unfairly! I do wish I could help. But I suppose you will tell me that I am only a ghost." He looked miserable.

"Maybe the lady's future is brighter than you think!" I said, trying to cheer him up. In fact, Mr. Brock had told Ms. Scoggin all about the ending of this book just a day ago, and so I knew what I was talking about. But, as always, he pretended not to hear me.

"Things will get better," Ms. Scoggin said, patting Mr. Brock's hand. "I am sure of it." She attempted to pick up her teacup. I watched her fingers pass through the handle several times before she managed it.

"I hope you are right," Mr. Brock said. "A ghost can only hope, I suppose." He gave a long sigh. "What courage!" Then he paused, and a suspicious look came over him. "But, Ms. Scoggin, I suddenly have the strangest feeling that I have read this book before." Mr. Brock's shoulders slumped. "I have no doubt told you all about it? Before?"

Ms. Scoggin and I exchanged a look.

"And I have listened with such joy, every time!" she said.

Mr. Brock used to remember every book he read. I had fetched hundreds of them over the years, from the library in Grantville. But recently he has begun to read the same story again and again, without even noticing.

"But how wonderful, Mr. Brock," I said quietly, "to be

able to read the books you love most, as if for the first time! I am quite jealous."

He is very good at pretending that he neither sees nor hears me. But he sat up a little straighter, gazed at Ms. Scoggin, and managed to produce a small smile. "I am a lucky man," he announced.

Ms. Scoggin's forehead was tight. She looked almost distressed.

"Is he all right?" I whispered.

"My dear," she said in a low voice, "this cannot go on forever, you know." She gestured impatiently. At the table? At ourselves, sitting around it? I wondered if she was unhappy with my dinner. I had served baked potatoes for several nights in a row.

"What cannot go on?" I asked her. "Are you talking about Mr. Brock's books, or the potatoes?"

"Potatoes!" She exploded. "What does this have to do with potatoes? I am talking about *us*. We can't stay much longer, my dear!"

Whenever she starts talking like that, I pretend not to hear her. I learned how from Mr. Brock.

They went to bed early, while I stayed up worrying (and washing the dishes). It was painful to see Ms. Scoggin so upset. But it's hard to solve a problem when you don't know what it is.

Today, I woke up determined to make the day a good one. I fixed Ms. Scoggin's tea, put two sugar cubes on her saucer, climbed the stairs, and knocked on her door.

"Come in!" she barked.

I put on an extra-large smile and entered her room.

She was sitting up in bed, fiddling with her pin.

"It won't stay on straight!" she said. "Impossible thing!"

Gently, I took it from her and fastened it to her shirt. "There," I said. "It's perfectly level! And here's your tea."

She sighed. "Thank you, my dear. I'm just a bit tired today."

Her librarian pin, from our library days, an impossible thing? I had never once heard her complain about it before. I touched two fingers to my own pin and hoped this was not another Changed Thing.

As I was closing Ms. Scoggin's door behind me, I heard two quick knocks from below. My heart jumped, and I rushed down the stairs and opened the front door.

No one. Just a small paper bag. I scooped it up.

I knew what was in the bag: a tuna fish and dill pickle sandwich on rye bread, with lettuce. In my library days, it was my favorite lunch. The sandwich arrives every Wednesday, but I am never quick enough to see who has left it for me.

I carried it, smiling, to the icebox. But then I thought, what's wrong with tuna for breakfast? (Especially after a week of potatoes?) So here I sit, eating it, and thinking about the dear boy again. It must be because of all the fuss about the library pins.

One day, long ago, when I was still getting to know him, I asked Ms. Scoggin for some advice. Could I be doing more to draw the dear boy out? To make him want to sit with us on the rug during Wednesday Book Club?

Ms. Scoggin said, "His mother died last summer. My advice is to let him sit where he wants to."

"Oh," I said. And she gave me an understanding look.

As Ms. Scoggin knew, I was also motherless. In fact, I had no memory of a mother or a father. At the orphanage, it had sometimes been said that those of us without parent memories were the lucky ones. But I was never sure about that.

It's true that I did not long for my parents, the way some others did. But aren't "parents" the source of a life's direction? If life is a line, leading somewhere, aren't parents the dot from which it sets forth?

Even people who disliked their parents, as one or two of my orphanage friends claimed to do, had a "from."

But me?

I was told that I could make up my own "from."

"Imagine whatever you like!" the orphanage manager told me. "Any of it could be true. Anything!"

But I did not know where to start. Were they farmers? Acrobats? Doctors? Spies? Sailors? Horse people?

Were they kind? Careless? Selfish? Brave? Horrible? Wonderful?

I would lie in bed, imagining. It was hard work. I preferred, once I had been taught how, to read stories that other people had imagined.

First, I read all the stories in the book room at the orphanage, and then I found all the other places books were hiding in the building. Our cook had a wonderful collection in her bedroom—she had kept every book she loved as a child. I worked my way through her shelves while "helping" in the kitchen, which meant occasionally stirring the soup with a spoon in one hand while holding a book with the other.

Then, in third grade, I discovered the public library. There were, I realized, many, many books to be read. (Until then, I had been slightly worried about running out.) At the orphanage, each of us had a flashlight, and I began to stay up very late with mine, reading until my eyes would not stay open. Which meant that I usually did not manage to turn my flashlight off. Luckily, I knew where the batteries were kept.

And then the orphanage manager found me rooting through the battery drawer, which was almost empty. She told me, gently, that I would need to start getting my own batteries.

"Let's go to the battery library, then," I told her. "I'm going to need a lot."

She laughed. "The *what*?"

"The *battery* library," I insisted, shaking my flashlight at her. "To borrow *batteries*."

There were no battery libraries. Batteries had to be bought with money. Batteries, she explained, were expensive. And once you were done with them, that was it, they were used up.

For the first time, it occurred to me that books *don't* get used up. Books got powered by the reader, didn't they? They could be read again and again. (As long as no one dropped them into the soup. Which only happened once.)

But I still needed batteries.

The manager said that I had given her an idea. She

would lend me battery money now, and I could pay her back later.

"How?" I asked her. "I don't have any money to pay you back with."

She said I would get a job, when I was older. Since I liked books so much, maybe I could get a job at a library. And that is what happened.

My first job was at our city library, an old, very large, not-too-clean building squeezed between a small bank and a smaller hardware store. To me, that library always looked like a grubby giant whose arms had been tied behind its back. My job was after school, because I was only thirteen years old. Mostly I mopped and looked with great longing at the young adults who stamped the circulation cards, wheeled around the squeaky carts full of books, and talked to the patrons. (About books!) They were, I learned, *assistant librarians.*

I mopped. And cleaned toilets. Nobody talked to me.

But I had library privileges. And battery money.

Chapter Seventeen

MORTIMER

The second major expansion of Martinville's little free library took the form of an old red wagon pulled by two third graders: Jessica and Winnie D. (Not to be confused with Winnie R., Mortimer remembered, who was in the fifth grade.)

Jessica and Winnie D. had divided their wagon of books into three parts and labeled them with beautiful handmade signs: There were HORSE STORIES, DOG STORIES, and OTHER ANIMAL STORIES.

No CAT STORIES. Mortimer tried to glare at them, but they were scratching him behind the ears at the time, and he did not manage it.

As they left, Winnie called back to him. "I'm coming back later, cat! With my dad!"

When the sun began to get low in the sky, Mortimer stretched out on the grass and listened to the frogs, who had started their night singing early. Several of the animal books had already been taken (two dog, one horse), and a few books had been added to the egg crate. Even with a few other afternoon departures, there wasn't much room behind the cheese cupboard doors. But all was well with the library.

He watched the door of his house, wondering when his dinner would emerge.

The porch door opened. Looking left and right, left and right, Al came quickly across the green with Mortimer's supper dish. Mortimer stood up and got ready for her hug.

But Al didn't hug him. She seemed entranced by the library.

"Look at this," she whispered, "the library is growing!" She examined the red wagon, her fingers caressing one book at a time while she cooed over the signs the girls had made.

Mortimer began to wonder if Al was going to set down his food dish anytime soon.

"Sorry!" she said, catching his expression. "I guess I got excited."

First looking around to make sure they were alone, Al sat with him while he ate. "Ms. Scoggin is hovering more than usual," she told him. "Last night, she had to keep hold of her chair with one hand in order to stay at the table! And Mr. Brock keeps dropping his books. I wonder if I should be worried. Are there ghost *doctors*, do you suppose? How would I even call one?"

Mortimer had never thought about it. Cats could see ghosts, of course, but he had never seen a ghost doctor. Then his thoughts were interrupted by voices from the other side of the green. Not mouse voices. Human ones.

Al's eyes got big. She hugged Mortimer quickly before picking up his empty dish. It was a tight hug on a full stomach, but Mortimer was happy to have it. Then he watched Al race back to their house, half-bent into a funny crouch.

The human voices approached from the other direction. Winnie D. was back, Mortimer realized, with her dad.

"Did you see *that*?" Winnie said, looking toward the History House, where Al had just scurried up the steps.

"Yes, I did," her dad answered quietly.

"Have you ever talked to her, Dad? Jessica tried once, on a dare. But the lady ran away."

"Don't play games with that lady," Winnie's dad said.

"If she wanted to talk to us, she would. I think she wants to be left to herself."

"Ooh, the cat's still there!" Winnie said, catching sight of Mortimer. "I told you he lives here."

Winnie's dad carried a big beach umbrella in one hand and a shovel in the other. He carefully dug a hole, inserted the umbrella stick, and then Winnie refilled the hole, patting the dirt down hard so the stick wouldn't wobble. When they opened the umbrella, it covered both Mr. Gregorian's egg crate and the red wagon. Then Winnie laid a towel, folded twice, on the ground under the umbrella.

"It's supposed to be a bed, if you want it," she told Mortimer.

After they left, he settled on the towel, which was nice and thick. From here, he could see all his books. He liked his bed very much. He doubted he would be able to see the stars through the umbrella, but he, along with the books, would stay dry if it rained.

Mortimer liked Winnie D. It was fine that she liked dogs and horses better than cats.

Mortimer liked his library. He was taking good care of it.

And so were the people of Martinville.

He wondered if Finn had ever found any food.

Chapter Eighteen

AL

I first saw the Martinville Library, and met Ms. Scoggin, the same week I started college in Grantville. I had just left the orphanage and was only seventeen years old. Everything felt very new and bewildering.

Ms. Scoggin had put an ad in the paper. She needed a "library helper," and she hired me on the spot. I hoped there would not be as much toilet cleaning in Martinville as there had been at the grubby giant.

Ms. Scoggin told me, soon after I arrived, that every time she read a new book, she built a new room in her mind. "I have rooms and rooms up here now," she said, tapping above her left ear, "but there's always space for another one."

After that, whenever I looked into her shining brown eyes, I imagined an enormous and beautiful house on the other side of them.

I had a pretty big house behind my eyes, I realized. But I wanted a bigger one.

For some years, I did very little besides go to my classes, clean the library, and read books. Sometimes, Ms. Scoggin helped me choose them. Hunched over my breakfast, riding the bus, and in bed with my flashlight, I built room after room in my mind.

My house grew very large indeed. And, slowly, I stopped worrying about the mystery of my "from." I did not have to imagine a tragic story about kind (but poor) acrobats, or smart (but selfish) bankers, because, I realized, I was "from" my own now-enormous house. The house I had built myself by reading all those books, with help from Ms. Scoggin, and from those flashlight batteries, which turned out to be, as the orphanage manager had promised, quite expensive.

It was only natural, once I had finally solved the question of my "from," to start to wonder about my "to." In other words, where was I going?

The answer was obvious. I was going to be a librarian.

When I told Ms. Scoggin, her face went bright. She walked to her desk, opened a drawer, and pulled out an application for library school.

She'd already written my name at the top.

Chapter Nineteen
EVAN

Evan's phone rang while he was brushing his teeth that night. He spit and ran back to his room without rinsing.

"I started thinking," Rafe said. "About what Mr. O'Neal said on the bus. And I looked up the library fire. Guess what? It burned down on the *exact same day* those books were returned. November 5, 1999. That's the date on all the circulation cards, right?"

"Yeah, are you sure?"

"It burned down *that night*, after closing. I found an article online."

Evan thought about the way Mr. O'Neal had been looking at him on the school bus.

"What started the fire?"

And why was Evan's heart pounding?

"I don't know." He heard Rafe clicking on his keyboard. "It just says *a fatal fire of unknown origin.* But there's almost nothing else about it online. All I could find was one PDF of a paragraph from an old paper. *Fatal fire.* That almost sounds like a title of an H. G. Higgins mystery, doesn't it?"

It did, actually.

Evan grabbed the journal lying on his bed, flipped to his mystery outline, and looked at the words "CRIME," "VICTIM," and "SUSPECTS."

Maybe this *was* that kind of mystery.

"Hello?" Rafe said. "You still there?"

"I'll call you back." He pulled *How to Write a Mystery Novel* from his backpack and found the Polaroid (which he'd been using as a bookmark).

His mom was right—it *was* like a really bad selfie. There was the corner of someone's glasses, half of one brown eye, and in the background, a town.

Now Evan realized why he hadn't recognized it as Martinville: There was an extra building in the picture. The library.

The picture was inside the book, and the book had

been returned to the library the very day it burned down. By H. G. Higgins. Way before he was famous.

The picture *was* a clue. It had to be. Was it H. G. Higgins in the picture?

On the day before the fire?

Evan tried to sleep, but trying to sleep was a joke. He switched on his light and picked up *How to Write a Mystery Novel* from the floor next to his bed. He was up to *Supporting Characters*, which didn't sound too scary. In fact, "supporting characters" sounded boring. Maybe they would help him get to sleep.

Supporting characters, the book said, included *everyone* the protagonist came into contact with during his search for the antagonist. Friends and family were supporting characters, and so were the people living and working in the town. His own mother was a supporting character, Evan realized. So was Mr. O'Neal. And Rafe, of course, along with every other kid in their class. That made him feel good. This mystery wasn't only about him. It was about all of Martinville.

But then he came to this line: "Remember! Your 'bad guy' will probably turn out to be one of your supporting characters, but won't be revealed as the bad guy until the end of the book."

He slammed the book shut.

What if the library fire had been started by someone he knew?

No. It couldn't be anyone from Martinville.

Because Evan couldn't imagine that.

But H. G. Higgins, or someone calling themselves that, had been at the library on the day it burned down. H. G. Higgins had returned this very book on the day of the "fatal fire." And then, as far as anyone knew, he had never come back.

Evan stared again at the Polaroid. At the brown half-eye. He was starting to feel like a real protagonist in a real story.

H. G. Higgins, Evan decided, was his number one suspect.

Tomorrow, he would look for more clues.

Chapter Twenty

AL

Not long after we created our secret book club, the dear boy and I conspired to rescue a mouse.

You have already heard, of course, about how mice sometimes like to come indoors, where there is warmth, food, and shelter from predators. Ms. Scoggin couldn't stand them. She said that the only place for animals of any kind in a library was "in stories." But she made an exception for the energetic gray-and-white library cat who helped keep out her number one enemies, the mice. (Years later, this cat became our own dear cat's mother. Ms. Scoggin was not pleased. In time, of course, she changed her tune.)

The dear boy, as I've said, was a Great Reader. He read a good number of books, and more importantly, he took some of them straight into his heart. One of those books was a story about a mouse. It changed him. After he read that book, he could no longer see mice as the enemy. He saw them as fellow creatures, just as many people see a puppy or a horse. And this was why the dear boy and I undertook our rescue. If I recall correctly, he called it Mission Mouse.

One afternoon, he came to me in an obvious panic. Refusing to explain, he led me into the rows of shelves under the balcony before stopping abruptly and pointing.

There was a space there, where the wood floor dipped a bit under the bottommost shelf. And in front of that space, as still as a statue and staring straight ahead with the intensity of a tiger on the hunt, was the cat.

That cat did her job well.

The first thing we did was shut the cat into the basement office. (The dear boy watched out for Ms. Scoggin while I did the actual deed.) Then we met back at the mouse hole. All was quiet.

"Wait," the boy breathed.

We waited.

In just a little while, a small nose appeared, along with some whiskers, a pair of small eyes, and some rather cute ears. The dear boy held out his hand, and the mouse approached. It was the color of a brown egg.

"You've been feeding it?" I whispered. If Ms. Scoggin discovered this, he would be banned from the library forever! "She will never forgive you," I said.

He explained that he could not help it. He loved this mouse, and it depended on him, just like the mouse in the book depended on his friend the mole. "We have to save him," he finished. "The cat will keep coming back until he gets him."

I hesitated.

"Like in the book," he repeated.

"Real life is not always like a book," I told him. "We don't want mice living here."

"That's why we have to move him somewhere else," he said.

I shook my head. But I couldn't say no.

And that is how, the following day, I came to spend eighteen dollars of my assistant-librarian salary on a cage, a bag of wood shavings, and a water bottle. All of it waited under my desk in a big bag until Ms. Scoggin went down to the basement office to sort the returned books. Then we moved fast.

The dear boy had brought some cheese and a glob of peanut butter in a plastic bag. The mouse was successfully lured.

"What will you tell your father?" I asked the boy, when we had closed the little cage door.

"What do you mean?" he asked, still smiling with the twin thrills of victory and relief.

"I mean"—and I pointed at the mouse, who was deeply engrossed in his snack—"where will you say he came from?"

He looked at me blankly. That was when I realized he meant for the mouse to come home with me.

"I have two dogs," he explained. "It would be horrible for him at my house."

That dear mouse lived with me, in my small apartment above the bakery, for the rest of his natural life. I named him "Eggy."

A week after Mission Mouse, I found what looked like a crumpled-up paper bag on my desk chair, tied around the middle with a limp green ribbon. Inside was a small carved wooden mouse. It had two tiny nail heads for eyes, and a glued-on skinny leather tail. I held it, understanding that I had been given a treasure. Ms. Scoggin had several treasures on her desk, collected over the years and displayed with pride. But this was my first. The dear boy!

The dear boy.

Chapter Twenty-One
EVAN

Thursday morning, Rafe was back on his corner, holding a can of bug spray. "Tuck your pants into your socks!" he shouted at Evan. "There could be ticks in there!"

"SHHHHH!" It was six thirty in the morning, and the whole reason they were out here this early was so that no one would see them. Evan stood not far away, covered in bug spray, confronted by a wall of thorny bushes. On the other side of it was the place where the Martinville Library had once stood. It was the best place he could think of to look for clues.

But it had looked a lot more "explorable" from the school bus window. Should he just push in? He wished for the thousandth time that his best friend was allowed to go places. It looked possible to get really lost in there.

But he figured that Rafe would at least tell someone to look for him, if Evan never came out. That was good.

"What are you waiting for?" Rafe shouted. Rafe always said that when he was finally allowed, he was going to do absolutely e-v-e-r-y-t-h-i-n-g, at least once. But that was easy to say.

Evan felt something move against his leg, and his heart gave a wild thump before he realized it was only the cat. Goldie. Sunshine. "Do you have a real name?" he asked the cat.

The cat gave him a three-part meow and then moved between his feet, rubbing his cheek against Evan's right sneaker, and then the left one.

Evan was really glad to see that cat, he realized. "Hi, cat," he said softly.

He felt a little better after that. He drew his thumb down his forehead, tightening his imaginary cap so that it wouldn't get pulled off by something in the thicket in front of him. And then he plunged into the wall of green.

He parted branches and leaves with his hands as he walked, slowly, trying to go in a straight line. He'd imagined a clearing, partway in, but couldn't see one anywhere.

It was hard to imagine that the big library Mr. O'Neal had described, which Evan pictured as almost a castle with large blue doors, could have stood right here. But his dad always said that if all the humans disappeared from Earth, pretty soon you would never even know they had been here, because nature was so powerful it would grow up over everything, pulling down the buildings and the bridges . . .

He sucked in his breath and stopped to disentangle himself from a skinny but viciously thorny branch that had attached itself to his sleeve. There was another one clinging to his sock. He bent down to pull it off. Were they trying to grab him? *No*, he told himself. Nothing was trying to grab him.

When he straightened up, all he saw were more branches and leaves, and he couldn't even remember which direction he'd been walking in. Why did this feel so impossible? Then, suddenly, the cat was there again, daintily stepping through the bush. He made a quick circle around Evan before setting off at an angle.

"Wait up!" Evan said, and followed the cat.

There *was* a clearing, just a few feet beyond where Evan had been standing. He felt his lungs expand the moment he stepped into it, took a deep breath, and said, "Wow."

There was a kind of ruin here, not like the ancient ruins they'd studied in Mr. O'Neal's class, but still a ruin. A stony foundation poked up here and there from the grass. Evan stepped up onto a crumbling chunk of it and, balancing, saw that if he could draw a line connecting all the stony parts, he would be looking at a big, empty square, with a cat sitting in the middle of it.

This was the library. He jumped off his chunk, into the square. The cat stayed put, head up and feet neatly put together, looking very much at home. "This is it!" Evan told him. "We're in the library!"

It *almost* looked like the cat nodded at him. Just once.

That's when Evan realized: There was no basement. He felt his heart drop. He'd known there wouldn't be a *building* here anymore, but he'd imagined that there'd somehow be a basement. The basement *where the fire had started*, according to that newspaper article Rafe found online. The basement where he'd hoped to find some clues. Or *one* clue, even.

"They must've filled it in," he told the cat. Evan walked all the way around the library's footprint, looking for clues. There were some blackened bits of stuff—metal? wood?—just tiny shards of unrecognizable things. He touched a few, but they were nothing. He did another loop around. He found an old dime. Nothing good.

The cat stayed right where he was, and even though

nothing felt exactly *scary*, Evan was glad he wasn't in there by himself.

Then he heard Rafe's voice. "ARE YOU OKAY?"

Evan smiled. Even if his legs did get hairy in middle school, Rafe would be there, too. Suddenly that seemed really, really good. He yelled back, "YES! I'M OKAY!"

But he was also ready to give up. He touched the scratches along his neck and wished he knew the fastest way out.

"DO ME A FAVOR!" he yelled. "CALL THE CAT!"

"DID YOU SAY 'CALL THE CAT'?"

"YES, CALL HIM!"

After a second, Rafe's voice boomed out, louder than ever. "HERE, SUNSHINE! HERE, KITTY-KITTY!"

The cat stayed where he was. Evan walked over, wondering if he should pet him. But not all cats liked to be petted, and Evan had been scratched up enough for one day.

"HERE, KITTY-KITTY-KITTY!"

The cat looked up at Evan, and then lifted one paw. There was something between his feet, Evan realized. Something that looked like . . . a ring?

Slowly, he dropped into a squat and reached for it.

"HEEEEEERE, SUNNY!"

Evan hadn't realized how loud Rafe could make himself.

But he didn't care about people seeing them anymore. He had found an actual clue. It *had* to be a clue.

"MR. KITTY CAT!" Rafe boomed. "COME!"

Almost as if he'd been waiting to hear his proper name, the cat rotated his ears, raised his tail, and started moving lightly toward Rafe's voice.

Evan followed, clutching two very dirty keys on a ring.

Chapter Twenty-Two

AL

I made apple pancakes for dinner, but last night's supper was no cheerier than the night before. Then, because his broom remains elusive, Mr. Brock spent the rest of the evening gathering dust balls with his fingers and flinging them out the front door (which I opened for him). Ms. Scoggin and I both watched him with concern until it was time for bed.

This morning, Ms. Scoggin came downstairs with her librarian pin stuck to her shirt with a great amount of tape. "It was the only way!" she said, slapping it with one hand. "The impossible thing will not stay on!"

The dear cat has stayed outside with my little library

for three whole days and nights now. Ms. Scoggin has stopped asking for him.

I feel the need to correct myself: The little library is not "mine." Libraries are meant to grow, and to be shared.

Perhaps it is time for me to explain how the little free library of Martinville came to be. Well, the "how" is simple: I built it.

This is the *why*.

Last Sunday morning, when I arrived with Ms. Scoggin's tea, she was already sitting up in bed with her "Librarian" badge pinned on and a dissatisfied look on her face. The moment she saw me, she sighed an enormous sigh and then started to tell me, once again, that it was time I "took my place."

First thing in the morning! Every morning! And me doing nothing wrong! Me just standing there holding her tea! Try, reader, to imagine twenty years of this sort of thing. Would you not sometimes lose your patience? Would you not?

I shouted, "What are you even talking about? Why is *this* not my place, just as it is yours? Is this *your* house? You are just greedy!" I was shouting. *At Ms. Scoggin.*

I expected her to shout back. She did not!

But she was surprised, I could tell. And—secretly pleased?

She said, "My dear, you are a librarian, are you not?"

"You know I am!" I was not done shouting, apparently. "Same as you are! But do you see me always telling you that you are in the wrong place? You do not!"

She stirred a sugar cube into her tea with a pinkie finger (ghosts are impervious to heat) and smiled at me. "I have Mr. Brock. You must find your *own* patrons, my dear."

I threw my hands up in the air. "There is no library! In case you have forgotten!" But I was not exactly shouting anymore.

She gave another sigh. "We must do with what we have." It was what she used to say in our library, when we ran out of binding glue or light bulbs. *We must do with what we have.*

"But we 'have' nothing, Ms. Scoggin. There was a massive fire, in case you have forgotten, and nothing is left. What am I supposed to do with *nothing*?"

She just looked at me.

In fact, we did not have *exactly* nothing left of our beautiful old library. We had a single library cart, and the books that happened to be on it that terrible night of the fire. But I was not sure how to be a librarian with one cart of miscellaneous books.

"And it is not *just* you," she said gently. "We are all in the wrong place."

I felt very confused, and knowing that my invisibility was probably at an all-time low, I hid extra well during the day's Sunday Tour, in the very back of the broom closet. As I waited there, barely breathing, with an old brass hook prodding the back of my neck, I reminded myself that Ms. Scoggin *was* my supervisor. I must consider her advice, repetitive as it was.

So, that night, I went to the basement, walked past the apples and potatoes, and stood in the farthest, dimmest corner, looking at the last library cart.

Just then, beside the cart, something moved. I'm not proud to say I let out a yelp, imagining a snake. At the sound of my voice, a furry face appeared—the dear cat! He very sweetly stood on one of my feet, asking for a hug.

And then, from my arms, he hopped lightly to the library cart.

I stared.

The dear cat was exactly where he had stood on the terrible night of the fire, when I pushed him (he was just a kitten then, barely bigger than my two fists together), along with the cart of books, out of the burning library basement. To safety.

This was after I had given up trying to find Ms. Scoggin in the smoke.

And before I finally found the dear boy.

I do not mention Mr. Brock because it was after-hours. I thought all the patrons had left and did not realize he was still there.

It was altogether strange to be looking at that library cart after so many years. Ms. Scoggin's words of that morning returned to me: *You are a librarian, are you not?*

And that is when it happened. An idea began to form in my mind: *I would build a new library.* (A very small one.)

It had been a long time since I'd had an idea. It felt very good.

I did not go to bed that night. Instead, I sketched. I measured. I marked. I gathered my tools.

And then it was time to wake Ms. Scoggin. I would need a lookout.

I never wondered, before the fire, whether ghosts need to sleep. They do. At least, we did. And some ghosts—like Ms. Scoggin—are very grouchy about waking up before dawn and being led to the basement before their morning tea.

"But why on Earth must you accomplish this task

before *sunrise*?" she said, wiggling her bare toes on the damp basement floor. (Ghosts are impervious to damp.) She knew all about my invisibility problems, so I did not answer by saying, "Because when I am out in daylight, people are often *seeing* me!"

Ms. Scoggin did not know that people sometimes even spoke to me, by accident. I can only imagine the long list of Criticisms she would have for a ghost who *talks* to people.

But if I had not answered them, I would have felt very rude. Instead, I used the fewest words possible and got away before anyone had time to understand that they were talking to a ghost.

"I thought you'd be pleased," I said to Ms. Scoggin, brandishing my hammer.

She looked curious and scanned the basement. When she saw the cart of library books before us, she suddenly scowled. "I do hope you plan to reshelve these books, my dear! Reshelving is a priority. Imagine a reader in search of a book finding only a blank space—as if some bully has knocked out a tooth!"

I reminded her, gently, that there was no library anymore.

"Oh, yes, yes," she said, waving at me impatiently. "I remember."

As I have said, the books before us, and the cart they sat upon, were all that were left.

"I am going to take care of these books," I told her. "It is time. That is my project."

"Good girl. How can I help?"

You could have knocked me down with a bookmark. Ms. Scoggin was offering to assist *me*? I felt quite emotional. But, in fact, that was exactly why I had brought her down there.

I asked her if she could whistle.

She could.

So we walked out into the night together. I pushed the cart over the grass, while the dear cat rode on top of the books, proudly facing front, as if he were sailing a ship.

Chapter Twenty-Three

EVAN

Evan thought it would feel a lot more satisfying to write "keys" on his list of clues. But it took only three seconds to write the word "keys," and only another four to realize that 1) he had no idea what to do with these keys, and 2) finding keys wasn't actually all that unusual. Now that he thought about it, he had found keys before.

Once, he'd found a key in the town hall parking lot when he'd gone with his mom to pick up their summer pass to the town pond. And once he'd found a set of three keys, on a braided pink-and-green cord, under a chair in the cafeteria at school. What had he done with those keys? Just turned them in, to the nearest grown-up. *Those* keys hadn't felt like mysteries. Maybe *these* keys weren't a mystery.

"What now?" Evan said, when he had escaped the thorns and shown the keys to Rafe. "We go around trying to fit these into doors?"

"I don't think that's legal," Rafe said. "And this one looks like it's for a padlock." He pinched the smaller silver key between two fingers.

"So we look for padlocks?"

Rafe thought. Then he said, "I'm not sure that's legal, either."

Things felt so different during the day than they did at night. With the sun shining, it seemed to Evan that the library fire was only a *possible* crime. Yes, there had been victims, but he couldn't think of a motive. And the book said that, in a mystery, the villain's motive was the second most important thing.

The *first* most important thing, the book said, was the ending: *Remember! If you are to satisfy your readers, justice must be done in the end.*

Evan liked the sound of that. He liked the sound of justice.

But maybe there was no villain, and no real mystery, here. Maybe not all of life was a mystery.

Even Mr. O'Neal could be wrong about things.

Mr. O'Neal's class had library on Thursdays. As they approached the door, Evan read, as he always did, the quote painted above it in rainbow letters:

We read to know we are not alone. —C. S. Lewis

Ms. Shore, the school librarian, told them that, in honor of the second-to-last day of school, it would be an "open class": They could talk without yelling, read on the floor, or get on the computers.

Everyone lunged for the computers—it was like a panicked game of musical chairs. Rafe somehow grabbed two right next to each other. Evan gave himself a celebratory spin in his chair before putting his fingers to the keyboard. He typed *H. G. Higgins*. And hit "search."

H. G. Higgins is a pseudonymous author of American mystery novels. His first book, Assignment Accepted, *was published in 2009, and he has published a bestseller every year since.*

"His first book wasn't published until 2009," Evan said.

Rafe looked up from a baseball-stats site on his computer. "Who?"

"H. G. Higgins. The book was returned on the night of the fire. In 1999. So there *was* no 'H. G. Higgins, the famous writer' when he borrowed that book. He was just H. G. Higgins, a random person!"

"Wow, yeah. It couldn't have been a joke—no one knew his name yet!" Rafe grinned. "I can't believe it. No one famous ever comes here."

"He *wasn't* famous, yet. That's the point." Evan was copying the information on the screen into his journal. "It doesn't say how old he is. If we knew that, we could figure out how old he was when he was here. Twenty years ago. What if he was a kid?"

"A kid called H. G.?"

"I guess? What if he lived here?"

"What does 'pseudonymous' mean?" Rafe said, frowning at Evan's computer.

"What?"

Rafe pointed. "The kind of writer it says he is."

"Oh—I don't know."

Rafe put his fingers on his keyboard. "Spell it for me."

Evan spelled it from the screen.

Rafe clicked. "Okay . . . whoa."

"What?"

"It means that H. G. Higgins is a fake name. A pen name, it's called. For when the author wants his identity to be a secret."

"A *secret*? That makes no sense. If you were famous, wouldn't you want people to know?"

"Yeah. And why would someone need a fake name ten years *before* he became famous?"

"I don't know," Evan said.

Although he could think of one reason. Maybe, before *writing* mysteries, H. G. Higgins had decided to create one in real life. By starting a fire.

Evan had the feeling he wasn't going to get an answer to his letter.

Evan found Ms. Shore, the librarian, reading a magazine at her desk.

"Where can I look up the real name of someone who is pseudonymous?" he asked, pronouncing it *soo-doh-NY-mus*.

"It's pronounced soo-DON-uh-mus. And it depends. Sometimes it's common knowledge, sometimes it's not," she said. "Who are you wondering about?"

"H. G. Higgins. I need to know his real name."

"H. G. Higgins? You want to know *his* real name?"

"Yes. He writes mysteries."

"I am aware of that. But I'm wondering how you can be so sure that H. G. Higgins is a *man*."

Evan blushed. "Oh. I just thought—"

"Exactly. You *assumed*. But you don't know. And neither do I. Actually, I don't know anything about H. G. Higgins, except that H. G. Higgins is probably very rich."

"I think maybe he—or she—lived around here, a long time ago."

"Really? That's interesting."

"Is there someplace I could look? To find out if he really lived here?"

"Without his real name? Can't think where. We certainly don't have anything here. And I doubt there's anything on file at the History House. They only have a few things—just town history, mostly. I don't think this qualifies."

Town history. "Do you think they might have newspaper articles about the library fire?"

She nodded. "Oh, yes. There's got to be *something* about the fire over there." Then she leaned back in her chair and squinted at him. "Your father is Edward McClelland, right?"

"Yes. Why?"

"He used to work there, that's why."

"At the History House?"

"No. At the library. When we were in high school."

"You know my dad?"

"Well, I did. When we were kids, we were in a book club together." She paused. "Sort of."

Evan went back to Rafe, who was now doing tomato research at his computer.

"No information," he told Rafe.

"We'll figure it out," Rafe said, scribbling notes about slug deterrents. "I'll be a lot more useful tomorrow."

"Tomorrow?" Evan repeated.

"Of course. Tomorrow we graduate."

"And?"

Rafe grinned at him.

"Do you mean . . . the *expiration date*?"

"We're graduating, aren't we? That means we won't be in elementary school anymore. We'll be *middle schoolers*."

Evan still didn't share the excitement about being *middle schoolers*.

But he was happy for Rafe.

Little known truth: Rafe was brave.

In fact, it was Rafe's bravery that had made his parents so worried in the first place.

The pre-K kids at Martinville Elementary played in the pre-K yard, which had a fence around it so that no one could wander off. It was just a fenced-off grassy area with a lot of rubber balls, hula hoops, and a plastic playhouse in it. Everyone loved the playhouse. They climbed around inside, and on top, forcing themselves through the windows, inventing games, and assigning one another characters. For some reason, Evan was usually a "dad" or a "storekeeper." He'd *wanted* to be one of the many wild "little brothers." Or Spider-Man.

Anyway. One day, a great shrieking came from inside the playhouse during pre-K recess. Evan was standing at one of the windows (he was being an ice-cream man). The shrieking came from Bruce Melon, who had just sneaked in (he was being an ice-cream store robber) when he noticed a black snake coiled up in one corner. Evan and Bruce hurled themselves through the nearest windows and onto the grass outside while Rafe dived *in* through the door to investigate.

Seconds later, he emerged, holding the snake in both hands. He carried it all the way to the fence and lowered it down to the grass on the other side while everyone stared (even the teacher). "Garter snake!" he shouted. "A baby. I think he was trying to hide."

Rafe's parents made their first special rule for him that very afternoon. The rule was "No picking up snakes." Soon to be followed by many others.

"They're worriers," Rafe had told Evan. "They can't help imagining every bad thing that could happen. The rules make them feel a lot better."

So Rafe followed the rules. But, in third grade, he had asked his parents about an expiration date.

"Expiration?" His mother's forehead wrinkled instantly. "Is the milk sour? Don't drink it!"

One of the rules was never to eat or drink anything without first checking the expiration date on the package. In fact, that was where Rafe had gotten the idea.

"An expiration date for the *rules*," Rafe said. "Someday, I do want to cross the street by myself. And climb trees. And walk on the grass without shoes and socks on."

His parents looked uncertain. "Well, I guess the rules can't last *forever*." His father's forehead was *also* scrunched up now, as if he were imagining that Rafe might run straight out the door and start picking up snakes.

"But, if there is an expiration date, it should be *very* far away," his mom added.

"How about . . . middle school?" Rafe said.

Both of his parents relaxed visibly. "Middle school!" his

father said. "Yes. Very good. The rules will expire when you are a *middle schooler.*"

And his parents smiled at each other, because at that time, *middle school* seemed so far away.

Most of the kids at Martinville Elementary had forgotten all about the snake. Evan had not forgotten. He knew that when Rafe did not cross streets and did not climb trees, he was only taking care of other people (his parents, this time). And Rafe didn't need anyone else to know it.

"Hey," Evan said, "so does this mean that *tomorrow*, after graduation, we can start looking for doors to open with the keys? Even if it's slightly illegal?"

"Tomorrow," Rafe confirmed, clicking over to a website called *Everything You Ever Wanted to Know About Fertilizer but Were Afraid to Ask.* "Right after I get back from the dentist."

Chapter Twenty-Four

AL

It took only a few hours to construct my little library. While I worked, Ms. Scoggin acted as my lookout, and the dear cat was her assistant. As the sky grew light, Ms. Scoggin began to sigh and ask about breakfast, but I was very firm that breakfast would be afterward. And she was a good lookout. Twice, she whistled, and I had just enough time to hide behind some bushes, leaving my work in a pile while someone passed along Main Street. Luckily, it was still too dim for most people to notice a pile of boards and books on the town green, and no one came to investigate.

My project turned out well. Even Ms. Scoggin approved. "I do miss *our* library, though." She had a sad look.

"I miss it, too," I told her. "Very much."

"A library is the place for you," she said as we walked toward home. "A nice *big* one."

"And leave Martinville? Who would take care of you and Mr. Brock?"

"Mr. Brock and I will do just fine," she said. "Just as soon as you take your place in the world. Perhaps this is a start." She smiled at me. I waited for a Reminder or a Criticism. But she continued to smile.

We had climbed up to our porch, where I dropped my saw, my hammer, and my extra nails.

"Thank you for your help," I told her. And I extended a fist to the dear cat, who rubbed his cheek against my knuckles. I held the front door open for him. (Ms. Scoggin had no use for doors, of course.)

But the dear cat would not come inside. Nor did he settle himself on the swing. The dear cat, who had never before ventured out alone beyond the top step of our porch, was now trotting down the stairs and marching off, tail up, back toward the town green.

"Cat!" Ms. Scoggin cried out. "Cat!"

But he did not even turn around.

"He'll be back soon," I said, but to be honest, I was shaken.

"I'll start getting breakfast ready," I said.

"Isn't it Monday?" Ms. Scoggin began to count on her fingers. Mondays were the day I visited Grantville, to renew Mr. Brock's book, buy our few necessities, and practice my invisibility. But I felt worn out. I watched her count and hoped she would not do it correctly.

"It is Monday!" she announced triumphantly. "You will do your errands. And *I* will fetch breakfast for Mr. Brock and myself."

"You? In the kitchen?"

"Go upstairs to change," she said, waving me toward the stairs. "And then you may take the last apple muffin to eat along the way."

She had a very generous look on her face, and so I thanked her, although of course I had made the muffins myself.

Chapter Twenty-Five

MORTIMER

Mortimer's fourth day as guardian of the library was momentous.

Early in the morning, the boy with the question-mark face appeared with his very loud friend. As things turned out, Mortimer's help was needed. The boy with the question-mark face got himself quickly turned around in the high bushes near Mortimer's beloved lost library, and then had trouble seeing the only thing there of any particular interest. Mortimer stood upon it until the boy finally noticed.

"Thanks!" the boy had said.

"You are welcome," Mortimer said. In truth, he was feeling quite overwhelmed by memories of Petunia. There was no library anymore, but Mortimer had been standing exactly where the old blue doors had once been. And those blue doors would always remind him of his fierce sister, Petunia, because of the time she got stuck on top of them.

He could almost hear her voice. "Chase me, Mortimer. Chase me!"

All your fault, his heart said.

And then, Mrs. Anne Baker, whom Mortimer knew well, brought her daughter to the little free library. A small suitcase swung from Mrs. Baker's hand. Her daughter held her other hand, although she could mostly walk by herself now.

"Hello, friend," Mrs. Baker said to Mortimer. "I heard you were the guardian of our new library. I brought you something." She held out a kitty treat. She often brought him a few when she led tours at the History House.

"Thank you," Mortimer said.

"You're welcome," she said. Mrs. Baker always seemed to know what Mortimer was saying. He liked that.

"Book!" Mrs. Baker's daughter said. She dropped her mother's hand and pointed with both hands—one aimed at the red wagon full of books, the other one at Mr. Gregorian's egg crate.

"Yes, sweetie. Books!"

“Book!” the girl repeated, now pointing at Mortimer.

Mrs. Baker laughed. “That’s a cat. Me-ow.”

From the small suitcase, which she had opened on the grass, Mrs. Baker removed a folded blanket. She shook it out and they settled on it: Mrs. Baker, her daughter, and Mortimer. That’s when Mortimer saw what else was in the suitcase: more books.

Everything was nicely arranged, with the small book spines all facing up. And inside the top of the suitcase, the word “POETRY” had been painted in big letters and surrounded by several small paint handprints.

“Paint!” the little girl said, pointing. “Paint more, Mommy!”

“Our paints are at home, honey. Let’s read now. Read book?”

“Book,” the girl confirmed. “Me-ow.”

Mrs. Baker removed one of the books from the case and opened it.

“Here’s a poem I love,” she said. “This poem is called ‘April Rain Song,’ by Mr. Langston Hughes. He was a teenager when he wrote it.” She cleared her throat, and began:

Let the rain kiss you.

Rain kiss! Mortimer thought. That reminded him of "wind tickle."

Let the rain beat upon your head with silver liquid drops.

Silver liquid, his heart said. *Yes! Exactly*.

Mortimer closed his eyes so he could listen better.

When the poem was over, he opened them. Something inside him had changed.

Listening to poetry, Mortimer's heart said, *feels like looking in a mirror*.

Maybe he *was* good with words, in his own way.

He wished he could tell Petunia.

"Whoops," Mrs. Baker said.

Mortimer looked up and saw clouds, heavy and low. He felt a few drops of rain.

Mrs. Baker closed the book and carefully pushed the suitcase along the grass until it was tucked safely under the umbrella. They all scooched until they were underneath, too. Together, they watched the rain fall. *Silver liquid drops*.

But Mortimer felt unaccountably tired. He knew he was old, but he had hardly ever *felt* old. Now he did.

If Petunia is anywhere, he told himself, *she must be old, too*.

Which seemed impossible.

Mrs. Baker left the suitcase, which became the library's fourth room.

Chapter Twenty-Six
EVAN

Friday morning, Evan's parents made him a special graduation breakfast, French toast with bananas. His mom squeezed fresh orange juice, and his dad cooked the bananas with sugar in a pan, making them sweet and crunchy. When they were sitting at the table, his parents looked pretty happy. His mom had actually taken her headset off, and his dad was laughing. Maybe, Evan thought, he should stop trying to solve a mystery that probably didn't exist.

He tried not to wonder about H. G. Higgins.

He tried to worry about nothing other than keeping his button-down shirt clean for graduation that afternoon.

* * *

He was stuffing books into his backpack near the back door when his mom asked, "Have you been back to the little free library, Ev? I drove by yesterday—people sure seem to love it."

Evan hadn't been back. He could see it across the street on his way to school, though. It was definitely growing.

His dad said, "I'd like to see it, too. Maybe after graduation?"

"It's weird they never rebuilt the *real* library," Evan said. "Why didn't they?"

His mom cleared her throat. "Well, when the library burned down, it was a really painful time—for the town."

"Dad? I mean, you *lived* here." His mother had grown up in California. She and his dad had met in college. "Didn't anyone want to rebuild it?"

His dad was staring at the table. He said, "If anyone did think about rebuilding, I'd be the last person in town they would talk to about it."

The kitchen felt quieter than it had ever been. Even the refrigerator seemed to hold its breath.

Evan said, "Why?"

But his dad just smiled. "I don't know why I said that, Evan. I guess I didn't get much sleep."

"The school librarian said you used to work at the

library, when you were in high school. Were you working there when it burned down? Did you know those people who died?"

His dad looked at the floor. "I have so many emails to answer, Evan. I can't have this conversation right now. I'll see you at graduation."

"Yes, the picnic!" his mom said, fiddling with the headphones that hung around her neck. "Dad's making a pie." She was nervous, Evan realized.

"You guys!" Evan said. "You can't just—not tell me anything!"

His parents studied him. The way they were looking at him made Evan feel, for those few seconds, like he could see himself through their eyes. He stood tall and looked right back at them.

Then his dad looked up and said, "You're right, Evan. How about after the picnic you and I talk? We can walk home together."

Evan hesitated. "This afternoon? You won't back out?"

"No chance. It's a plan. So get yourself on the road, and let me do my work and start up this pie."

Evan glanced at his mom, who was smiling across the kitchen at his dad. His dad would explain it all. Today! Why hadn't he just asked him before?

He left the house feeling closer than ever to solving his probably-not-even-a-mystery.

The day felt long, even for a half day. Evan mostly looked around their classroom and felt weird that they were never coming back to it. He couldn't even eat his lunch, but he wasn't sure if it was because he was excited about graduating, nervous about talking to his dad later, or sad about leaving Martinville Elementary. Through the cafeteria windows, they started to hear cars pull up. The families were coming.

Mr. O'Neal excused himself, and everyone knew why. Every year, he bought a new bow tie for graduation, and he always put it on right before the ceremony started. The ties were usually . . . colorful.

"What do you think it'll be?" Evan asked Rafe, who was eating Evan's sandwich. "Polka dots? Rainbow stripes?"

Rafe chewed. "Baseballs, maybe?"

"Baseballs?"

Then Mr. O'Neal reappeared, wearing a bow tie with little books on it. Some of the kids clapped. "In honor of our new little free library," he said, patting his tie. "This is it! Graduation time. Let's line up."

Then the other fifth-grade teacher, Ms. Brennan, called out, "Let's move, people!" and her class jumped up and mobbed the door. Mr. O'Neal rolled his eyes.

Chairs had been set up on the lawn outside, and it was sunny out, with what Evan's mom liked to call a "perfect breeze." While they marched down to their seats near the front, kids waved to their parents and pointed at the rows of desserts waiting on the long table near the podium. Evan found his parents and waved. Then he caught up to Rafe in line so they could sit together.

Each year, the fifth-grade teachers picked poems to read at graduation. This year it was Mr. O'Neal's turn to read first. "This year's graduating class is an especially lovely and deep group of students," he said, unfolding a piece of paper. "So I picked an especially deep and lovely poem. It's called 'The Summer Day,' and it was written by the American poet Mary Oliver."

He cleared his throat, and began:

"Who made the world?
Who made the swan, and the black bear?
Who made the grasshopper?
This grasshopper, I mean–

the one who has flung herself out of the grass,
the one who is eating sugar out of my hand,
who is moving her jaws back and forth instead of
up and down–
who is gazing around with her enormous and
complicated eyes.
Now she lifts her pale forearms and thoroughly
washes her face.
Now she snaps her wings open, and floats away.
I don't know exactly what a prayer is.
I do know how to pay attention, how to fall down
into the grass, how to kneel down in the grass,
how to be idle and blessed, how to stroll through
the fields,
which is what I have been doing all day.
Tell me, what else should I have done?
Doesn't everything die at last, and too soon?
Tell me, what is it you plan to do
with your one wild and precious life?"

Mr. O'Neal looked up from his paper, smiled, and blew them all a kiss.

"Wow," Rafe said.

Evan turned around in his chair to look at his parents.

His dad was wiping at his eyes. He saw his mom lean over to kiss him on the cheek.

Then Ms. Brennan was marching up to the podium. She grabbed it with both hands and leaned forward.

"Life is like riding a bicycle!" she shouted. "To keep your balance, you must keep moving! Albert Einstein said that!" She turned around and walked back to her seat.

Then the fifth graders stood up to get their diplomas, one by one. Mr. O'Neal stood off to the side and shook hands with every kid in their class. When it was Evan's turn, he said, "Keep looking for life's mysteries, kid."

And that was it. Everyone turned their attention to the dessert table.

There were sixty different kinds of cakes, pies, brownies, and cookies.

Correction, *fifty-nine*: Rafe's parents had brought a bag of mixed nuts, because they "worried about sugar."

Plus, they said, Rafe had that dentist appointment right after the picnic.

"Do they remember about the expiration?" Evan asked Rafe. They were on a blanket, eating five kinds of cookies. And this was only round one.

Rafe shook his head. "I have a feeling they forgot all about it. But it's probably better that way."

"Yeah, they look nice and relaxed." Squinting, Evan had picked out Rafe's parents in the crowd standing around the long dessert table. "Your parents only moved here ten years ago, and they're talking to everyone. Look at my dad, alone over there. And he was *born* here."

Evan's dad was, as usual, standing a little bit apart from everyone else.

Rafe said, "He's just shy, maybe." He shoved a whole cookie into his mouth.

Half an hour later, Evan walked around picking up stray napkins and feeling antsy to leave. He was uncomfortably full of dessert, but worse, his dad had promised (promised!) to tell him . . . *something*, on the way home.

And then, when everyone had started gathering up their blankets and packing up their half-eaten pies, his dad had totally backed out.

"I'm so sorry, Evan."

"Dad! You *promised*."

Looking upset, his father was already moving toward the parking lot. "I just—I can't right now. But we'll talk soon. I promise."

Evan stared after him. What just happened? A minute ago, he'd looked like he was actually having fun, for once, laughing with Mr. O'Neal. And then, when it was finally time to walk home together, he ran away.

Evan was done with waiting. It was time to put his detective cap on again. But he didn't draw his thumb down his forehead. Too many people around.

Evan kicked a napkin. Then, feeling bad, he bent down and picked it up. His mom came up behind him and put an arm around his shoulders. "Your dad just needs a little more time. Walk me home? I'll buy you a piece of pie."

"Not funny. And I can't go home yet. I have something to do."

"Okay. But be home for dinner." His mom raised the basket in her hand. "We're having pie!"

Chapter Twenty-Seven

AL

Another graduation day.

The poems were especially good this time. (I listen every year, from the corner of our porch.) And the sight of the children running like wolves to the dessert table is always cheering. But when I came back inside and closed the door behind me, all my worries returned.

Ms. Scoggin is often off the floor now, for one thing. Hovering.

Mr. Brock reads the first chapter of his book over and over.

And the dear cat does not come home.

And me. I feel different, too. That old library cart carried not just old books, but old memories. Strong ones.

Mr. Brock's singsong voice came down the stairs. "Ms. Scoggin? Where, oh where, is my 4:00 P.M. cheese, Ms. Scoggin?"

"I'm sure I have no idea!" Ms. Scoggin called back to him from her chair in the parlor. "But I hope it arrives soon, along with my tea!" She hovered above her chair, grabbed on to the seat cushion to steady herself, and fixed me with a look.

I was very happy to make the tea and fetch the cheese because I wanted—well, what did I want?

For Ms. Scoggin's smile to come back, mostly.

So I brewed a pot of tea and brought it to Ms. Scoggin, and then took the cheese plate from the kitchen cupboard and set off for Mr. Brock's room with it.

I was rushing past the front door on the way to the stairs when I heard a knock.

Someone was at the door. On a Friday.

Someone, I realized, who could definitely *see* me.

Was it just bad luck that I had been right in front of the big porch window?

It was a boy, holding a notebook.

As you know, my invisibility has always been a struggle. I could tell that it was doing absolutely nothing for me now.

Because the boy was waving to me through the thin curtain, just a little.

I had two choices. I could pretend I had not seen him, and just turn my back and walk away, or I could open the door. Neither one appealed to me at all. It's terrible when you don't like your choices. I looked at the cheese, and then back to the boy, who gave me a little smile. I have never in my life been able to turn my back on a smile.

Which meant that I would have to open the door. So I did.

"Hello," he said uncertainly. "I don't know how this works. Was I supposed to make an appointment?"

"Yes," I said. "I believe all History House appointments are to be made *in advance*. And tours are on *Tuesdays and Sundays*." I thought of all my best hiding places, and how far I was from them.

His smile dropped, and he said, "Oh. Sorry." And suddenly I was looking at the schoolbag on his back. He clearly intended to walk away, and if I'd had a moment to reflect, I would have let him do just that. Instead, some long-buried instinct kicked in, and I heard myself speaking!

"Wait. How can I help you?"

Chapter Twenty-Eight
EVAN

The woman who opened the door at the History House was not the same one who gave the tours. Evan felt kind of silly when he realized he had assumed that Mrs. Baker, who also worked at the Martinville Town Hall and ran the Summer Pancake Breakfast at the firehouse, actually *lived* at the History House. That was silly, like when he was little and thought that his teachers lived at school.

Instead, he stood in front of a barefooted lady in a long summer dress holding a plate of cheese. She wore a small round pin below her collar that said "AL." And she did not look happy about opening the door.

She looked . . . nervous. And told him he was supposed

to make an appointment, which he was almost relieved to hear. He turned to go.

But then she said, "Wait. How can I help you?"

He turned back. Now she was smiling. He couldn't help looking at the cheese, arranged in four small, perfect triangles. Maybe there was a party going on in there? Someone had probably rented the History House for their own private graduation party. That would explain the name tag.

She followed his gaze, glanced at the plate, and said, "Oh, I'm sorry. I wish I could offer, but someone's already—this belongs to someone." She blushed.

Evan felt himself go red, too, and said, "Oh, no, I don't want any. But are you having a party? I can come back."

She laughed. "A party! No. This is just—" She moved her cheese-plate-hand behind her back. "Never mind. Please come in!"

Evan had been inside the History House many times over the years—it was always open on town holidays, like the Winter Stroll, when everyone bundled up and walked around the green admiring all the lights people put up on their houses and trees. He and his mom always stopped at the History House, where the old iron chandelier was lit by a lot of small candles, and drank cups of hot cider while his dad waited outside. His dad always said it was too pretty out to come inside.

And Mr. O'Neal had brought them here for a Tuesday Tour, even though they'd already gone in fourth grade, and also in second grade. But Evan didn't mind—he loved seeing the way people in Martinville lived a hundred and fifty years ago—the rooms lit only by candles, pitchers and basins in the bedrooms for washing, big clunky wooden beds with beautiful quilts on them, and the kitchen where people had once cooked their meals inside the massive fireplace, which had an iron hook to hang the pots on. Each dish had its own slot in the wooden rack that hung on the wall. The cups hung on their hooks. There was something peaceful about all of it.

Now, from where he stood on the porch, Evan could see into the two front rooms, one of which was a cozy living room with a fireplace, a small sofa, and two soft chairs. The other room was mostly empty, except for a wooden table with chairs around it. This was where his class had gathered to listen to Mrs. Baker talk about the history of Martinville. She'd spread out some pictures and old papers on the table, and they all took turns looking. But not touching. Mrs. Baker had been very clear about that.

Today, the table was bare and gleaming, and Al the cheese lady was pulling out a chair for him. He took off his backpack and sat carefully with it in his lap. She wasn't looking at him, but she wasn't *not* looking at him. It was a little strange.

"Now, what sort of book are you after?" she asked.

"Oh. I'm not—*after*—a book," Evan said. "I thought there might be some old pictures here, that I could look at. Of the old library. Or maybe some newspaper articles, from back when it burned down?"

The cheese woman froze.

"I won't hurt them," he added. "I mean, I won't mess anything up."

She unfroze. "Don't worry about that. In fact, you look like a very careful person. And yes, there is a box of things, clippings and such. Can you wait right here? Will you be all right alone for a minute?"

When she came back, she had a pair of eyeglasses hanging by a thin chain around her neck and a cardboard box in her hands.

A half hour later, Evan was partway home, holding his journal tightly to his side. He hadn't wanted to put it in his backpack, because that would have meant letting it out of his sight. And he could not do that.

Inside his head, he could *hear* the words he had copied from the newspaper clipping, almost as if they were screaming at him:

The fire warden has determined that the tragic fire started in the basement. The police are questioning a young library intern, who was the last person known to have been in the basement before the fire broke out. His name is withheld here due to his age.

The road home felt much, much longer than usual.

Chapter Twenty-Nine
AL

What an extraordinary half hour. How can I explain it? To be *useful* again, not as a tea-and-cheese-bringer, or a potato-cooker and applesauce-maker, but, almost, as a librarian.

To be engaged with a young mind—a curious mind! It was wonderful. I felt I had to stop myself from floating up off the floor right in front of him (although I had never actually managed to float). For once, I was *grateful* for my unsatisfactory invisibility. That struggle, which I had always thought of as a weakness, had given me this beautiful moment.

I looked out the window and across the way, to where

my little library stood. I felt proud of our town for making it grow, and proud of the dear cat for watching over it. And I remembered Ms. Scoggin's words. *You are a librarian, are you not?*

Chapter Thirty
EVAN

Evan wasn't even halfway home when he heard a squeaky bike bell from the road behind him. Evan stopped and turned. Demetri Pappas was pedaling toward him with a big smile on his face, calling out, "Evan!"

When Demetri braked in front of him, Evan saw that his bike basket was full of individually wrapped brownies.

"Want one?" Demetri said. "I got over to the town green as soon as the bus dropped me off. So many desserts are looking for a good home on graduation day." He grinned.

"I'm full," Evan said, one hand on his stomach. *You're* tall *now*, he was thinking. In his running shorts, Demetri's legs looked a mile long. And he used to be kind of short. Like Rafe.

"I saw you guys at school this week," Demetri said. "You excited for Grantville Middle?"

"Yeah. I guess so."

Demetri laughed. "I wasn't thrilled about it, either. But you'll like it. You get to pick an instrument. And I'll be on your bus! For a year, anyway."

Evan tried not to be too obvious about it, but he was still looking at Demetri's legs. He had some bike grease on one shin, but his legs weren't *extra* hairy. For some reason, this felt reassuring.

"It's my other leg," Demetri said, raising his far knee.

"What?"

"The scar."

That was when Evan remembered Demetri's epic scar, which ran down one leg, from hip to knee.

And then he remembered how Demetri got it.

"I just realized that I forgot something," Evan said. "I have to go back to town."

"Okay—have a good summer. I'm leaving for camp next week." Demetri pedaled away, calling back, "I'll save you a seat on the bus in September, okay?"

"Okay! Thanks!" Evan was already running in the other direction, despite the stomachache. To Rafe's house. Because what he had to do next was dangerous, and he would feel better if Rafe were with him.

Luckily, Rafe's dentist appointments were usually very quick. His parents made him brush after every meal.

Chapter Thirty-One
EVAN

The treehouse was a little bit famous—to the kids who knew about it, mostly the kids who lived on Evan's road. It was just far enough into what they thought of as "their" woods that, when they first saw it, they imagined they had discovered something that not even one grown-up knew about. And the treehouse was high enough that they knew climbing up there was not only definitely against the rules, but actually pretty scary.

Then they got a little older. They talked about it, daring one another to go up. A few did go up, though none got in. There was a locked door, they reported, at the top of a very wobbly climb. The "ladder," just rough planks of wood nailed to the trunk every few feet, had chipped in many places, and a few spun unexpectedly on their nails. Everyone who went up seemed relieved to be safely back on the ground, with the exception of Demetri Pappas, who lost his grip, got a cut down one leg, and broke an elbow. He was two years older than Evan, and was the chief reason Evan was never tempted to go up there himself. Until now.

Demetri was a friend, but being two years older, he'd started taking the bus to Grantville Middle two years ago. He was in the middle school orchestra, and came home on the "activities bus," which got in later. He had a lot of homework and didn't hang out in the woods much anymore.

Evan looked up at the tree.

It was Demetri who had told Evan about the padlock on the treehouse door, after he fell. He had used the exact word Rafe had: *padlock*.

"Are you sure you want to do this?" Rafe asked. "My dad says this thing is an attractive nuisance."

"What instrument does Demetri play again?" Rafe's mother taught music to a lot of kids in town.

"Violin," Rafe answered.

Evan felt the outside of his front pants pocket to make sure the keys were still there. He tightened the straps on his backpack. "So his elbow must be fine now. If he plays violin, I mean."

"True," Rafe admitted. "Mom says he's very good, actually."

Evan nodded, put one foot on the first nailed-in plank, reached up to the second plank with both hands, tested it for stability, and hoisted himself onto the tree's trunk.

There were a few shaky moments, but Evan climbed, plank by plank, until his arms felt weak and his head was almost level with the metal latch on the treehouse door. As promised, there was a padlock on it. A padlock that had foiled every previous climber.

Grateful for the nice thick branch beside him, Evan braced himself and fished for the keys. "Don't drop," he heard himself say. But he wasn't sure whether he meant "don't drop the keys," or "don't drop to the ground." It was a long way down.

He grabbed the lock, which meant both hands were now off the tree itself, making him slightly light-headed with fear, and slid the smaller key into it.

"It FITS!" he yelled.

"YAY!" Rafe called back.

Evan smiled but didn't look down. He turned the key and heard a *click*. The lock popped open.

"It's unlocked!" he yelled, and then carefully maneuvered the padlock off the latch, shoving it into his pocket. He didn't want to drop it on Rafe's head.

Now all he had to do was open the treehouse door. He had to duck, to let it swing over his head. One arm wrapped around his friend (the sturdy branch), he gripped the corner of the door and yanked.

And then a few things happened very quickly.

First, Evan realized that the rusty hinges were not going to hold the door.

Also first, because these two things actually happened simultaneously, the door tilted dramatically, paused for a second, and then fell to the ground.

In that one-second pause, Evan had let go of the door so that he would not go down with it. He hugged his branch and heard the door land with a huge crash, followed by what felt like a huge silence.

Arms trembling, he hung there. "RAFE?"

More huge silence.

He looked down. But all he could see were leaves. "*RAFE?*"

Then he heard Rafe say, "Whoa."

"ARE YOU OKAY?"

"Yeah!" Rafe yelled. "It missed me!"

Evan felt his heart start up again. "I'm coming down!" he yelled.

"No, keep going!" Rafe called. "I'm on my way up!"

"What? No!"

"What, *yes*! Expiration date, remember? Get going—I'll be up there in a minute, and you'd better be out of my way!"

His eyes now at treehouse-floor level, Evan saw a rough plank floor covered with dirt and broken branches. He reached out, shoved his fingers into a crack between two floor planks, and pulled himself in. Flipping over, he lay there, looking up at . . . very little: plank walls with light shining in between the cracks, and a big open window covered by a screen of leaves hanging outside it.

He sat up. Everything felt pretty solid. He took a few deep breaths and was getting to his feet when Rafe's head popped up at the doorway.

"That was fast," Evan said. "I'm really glad you aren't dead."

Rafe smiled. "Me too. Pull me in—I need a hug."

He wasn't kidding. When Rafe needed a hug, he asked for a hug. It was one of the things that made Evan understand that Rafe, unlike Rafe's parents, was mostly fearless.

Once he was in, and after the hug, Rafe brushed shards of bark from his shirt. "The ground isn't as safe as my parents think it is."

They scoured the treehouse for clues.

They *tried* to scour it, anyway. It was just the floor, four thin walls, and a bench built in along one of them, opposite the overgrown window, which filled the treehouse with a strange greenish light.

No shelves. No boxes. Nothing else to open. Nothing to find.

"Not seeing any clues," Rafe said, running his fingers along the rough walls. Rafe had read that sometimes the hands could feel what the eyes missed. He jerked one hand back suddenly, but only to suck on a finger and say, "Ow. Splinter."

"Keep looking," Evan said, examining the underside of the bench. "Maybe there are initials carved somewhere. Look for *HGH*."

Squinting at his splinter, Rafe said, "Tell me again why this matters so much?"

Evan hesitated. "I need a suspect," he said. "A real one."

Rafe nodded. Then he said, "Tell me again why you need a suspect?"

"*Because.*" Evan took a deep breath and decided to say the words. This was Rafe. He could trust Rafe.

"Because *my dad* is a suspect. I think he was working at the library that night. In the basement, where the fire started. But he didn't do it. I know he didn't. So I have to figure out who did." He waited for Rafe to ask more questions.

But all Rafe said was, "Your dad would never set fire to a library. Not in ten million lifetimes. Anyone who knows him would know that."

It felt good to hear Rafe say that. "Yeah, well. Not everyone knows him, I guess."

"But you really think H. G. Higgins had something to do with it?"

Evan shrugged. "Maybe. We know he returned a book that day. A book with a picture in it."

"But we don't know that those keys were his. They could have been anyone's."

"The keys opened the treehouse," Evan said, sitting down on the bench. "So if there's something up here that points at H. G. Higgins, he'd be a *real* suspect. I could tell the police, maybe."

"Yeah. But there's nothing here." Rafe paced around the floor in a tight circle, then stopped in front of the single, overgrown window. Leafy branches hung every which way just outside it, blocking the view.

Evan stared for a second, then jumped up and went to the window. Reaching through the opening, he tried to push aside some of the branches. "Help me."

Even using all four of their arms, they managed to clear only a little spy hole through the green. But it was enough. All of Martinville lay below them. They could see most of the town hall, a corner of the school, and the top half of the History House.

Evan said, "This is it! *This* is where the Polaroid picture was taken. H. G. Higgins—or someone—was standing right here with the camera."

Rafe smiled. "The picture was inside the book . . ."

Evan reached for his backpack and felt around inside it. "And the book was returned to the library on the day of the fire . . ."

"By *H. G. Higgins*!"

Evan held up the Polaroid while Rafe did his best to maintain the view through the spy hole without falling through the window.

"Right here," Evan said. "I can even see that knot in

the picture." He pointed to a brown spot in the wood just beside the window.

Rafe squinted at the Polaroid. "Yeah. And whoever's eye that is. Too bad there isn't a little more face. This could be anyone." He held the picture up to Evan's face. "It could be you!"

"This *proves* that H. G. Higgins used to live in Martinville. He was at the library the day it burned down. And then he never came back. He probably lives in New York City with millions of other people and thinks no one will ever find him!"

"Suspicious," Rafe said. "But why would he want to burn down a library? He writes *books*."

"I'm going to find him," Evan said, ignoring the question. "I'll make him confess. And then everyone will *know* my dad didn't set that fire."

"I'll help you," Rafe said.

Chapter Thirty-Two

AL

The problem with my beautiful moment with our visitor was that I wanted the one after it to be beautiful, too. I wanted another person, a person with questions, to knock on the door. But the child with the notebook was only in the house for twenty minutes, and there was no one else.

After he left, I sat down at the big wooden table with the box marked "Martinville Library Fire." He had carefully repacked the things inside, which I appreciated as I laid them out in front of me. There were a few news articles from the Grantville paper, and even a short paragraph from the *City News*. (Martinville is too small to have its own newspaper.)

Plus the obituaries of Ms. Scoggin and Mr. Brock. (They had both led notable lives, unlike myself.) I remembered the funerals, where the three of us ghosts had stood together in the sunlight, watching. I was particularly watching our dear boy, of course. Though we'd watched him grow quite tall by the time he was a teenager, his cheeks had never fully lost their roundness. He still blushed whenever he spoke, which is a sure sign of depth and sincerity. And, at Ms. Scoggin's funeral, he spoke.

He talked about what the library meant to him. I know it sounds unlikely, but it *seemed* as if he was looking at us the whole time he spoke. I felt just as invisible as Ms. Scoggin and Mr. Brock were that day, but I may have been fooling myself.

My mind struggled with the same old knot:

1. It was impossible that our dear boy had started the fire. He would never do such a thing. Even if he was upset. Never.
2. It was impossible that anyone else had started the fire: The warden said that a match had been struck in the library basement and held to a book. No one but the dear boy had been there.

I remembered the dear boy that fateful evening, his head down and his ears bright red, hurrying down the basement stairs after Ms. Scoggin let him have it: Criticisms galore. He hadn't changed the paper towel rolls in the bathrooms. He needed to remember to stand up straight and look people in the eyes. And, worst of all, he'd mis-shelved some biographies in the fiction section! A misfiled book was as good as lost, didn't he know that by now?

By the time he got away from her, he was practically running.

I had not let myself think of that day for a long time.

I gathered up the clippings, put them back in their box, and walked it over to the large cabinet marked "Town History."

Hardly anyone ever comes to look at such things.

Lost in my cloud, I crossed the parlor to gather Ms. Scoggin's teacup.

She was in her chair, her cup within reach, but still full to the brim and, by now, surely cold. Mr. Brock had come downstairs and was in his spot on the sofa.

Or he was hovering above it, anyway. I stared: They were both hovering now? Why?

Mr. Brock gripped his book with both hands. I realized

I had never given him his cheese. It wasn't like him not to notice the absence of cheese.

"You didn't drink your tea," I said to Ms. Scoggin. "Should I brew another pot?"

She shook her head. "I shouldn't have yelled at him," she said. "He was a good boy." She covered her librarian pin with one hand.

I didn't say anything. I knew she wasn't talking about the child who had just left our house. We both knew exactly who she was talking about. The dear boy. But what could either of us do about it now?

I will always remember the day Ms. Scoggin presented him with his official staff pin. His eyes blazed with a pride I remembered from my own first day at the library. From that moment, he never came to work without it. We all wore our pins.

Ms. Scoggin's said "Librarian."

Mine said "AL" (for "assistant librarian," which Ms. Scoggin said was too many letters to fit.)

And Edward's said "Intern."

Edward. That was his name. Our dear boy.

He liked to call me Al.

Chapter Thirty-Three

EVAN

"Dad!" Evan wasn't even in the house yet. He was shouting from the driveway. "Dad!"

His father's worried face appeared on the other side of the cellar window, near Evan's feet.

"Dad!" Evan talked at the window. "I know about the library. I know what everybody thinks—that you . . ." He couldn't make himself say it.

His dad's face went away. Ten seconds later, his father banged out through the screen door with hard eyes and blotchy cheeks. "Who told you that?"

"No one told me!" Evan said. "I figured it out myself." He held up *How to Write a Mystery Novel.* "Everyone thinks you set that fire, don't they? But I know what to do—I think I know who did it!"

"Slow down," his dad said. "Start at the beginning."

"Why won't you *talk* to me?" Evan started to cry. Which he had not expected.

His dad's face changed. His shoulders relaxed, and he said, "I guess I haven't known *how* to talk about this with you. Let's go sit on the rock." He reached out, took Evan's hand, and led the way around back, to the big rock Evan's grandmother had named the "rock of truth" when his dad was little.

It was still warm from the sun.

"Upsetting you is the last thing I wanted, Evan," his dad started. "I didn't set the library fire, but I'm sure plenty of people still think I did. I was there that night. And I was questioned by the police, several times. It's not something I like to think about. I guess I hoped you would never hear about it. That was—unrealistic." He smiled, a little. "I should have been the one to tell you about all this. I'm sorry I didn't."

Evan waited. The first rule of the rock of truth was "no lying." The second rule was "no interrupting."

But his dad seemed to be out of words. Evan said, "The paper said the fire started in the basement. A match had been struck and held to a book."

Evan's father shook his head. "That's something I would never do. Never. But I was the only person there."

"Are you totally sure, though? That you were the only person there?"

His dad nodded. "But I didn't light any match. I was questioned, like I said. Word got around." He stopped.

"The article said there was an intern." Evan pointed at his father. "*You* were the intern?"

"Yes. After my mom died, going to the library . . . helped me. I felt safe there, like nothing bad could get me. When I was fourteen, the head librarian asked me if I'd like an after-school job, as a helper. I couldn't believe it—getting paid to be at the library? I told her yes. Her name was Mildred Scoggin, and she was a great lady. She was also a strict lady, and she was usually yelling at one of us—at me, I mean, or at the assistant librarian.

"Anyway, one afternoon she told me off about something or other, and then sent me down to the basement to deal with the book returns. The book-return chute sent the books down there, to a bin. I would replace the circulation cards, stack the books on a cart, and reshelve them.

"I'm sure I felt like an idiot for getting yelled at in front of everyone, but like I said, she was the boss, and she did a lot of that. But the police made a big deal about it, later.

They kept asking if I was *angry*. And I kept telling them, *no*, she was always like that. Al—the assistant librarian—called them Ms. Scoggin's 'Criticisms and Reminders.' We had kind of a joke about it. So going down to the basement to do the book returns, it really felt like any other day."

"But it wasn't any other day," Evan said.

"No. It was the day the library burned down."

"Did she—die? Ms. Scoggin?"

His father hesitated only for a moment. "Yes. Mildred Scoggin died of smoke inhalation."

"You got out, though."

His dad nodded. "Al saved me. She dragged me outside, through the basement door. But I know a lot of people around here still think I started that fire."

Evan was swept by a rush of anger. "How could you *let* them think it?"

His father looked sad. "I didn't 'let them' think it. I *always* said I didn't do it. But how could I prove what *didn't* happen, without knowing what *did* happen? I still have no idea."

"*I* believe you, Dad. I know you didn't set that fire. You *didn't*." Evan's eyes filled with tears of frustration. Possibly the worst kind of tears.

His father opened his arms, and Evan leaned into them. They sat like that for a while, while Evan's mind rushed around: *It was H. G. Higgins*, he thought. *He was there that day.*

The book, the Polaroid picture, the keys, the treehouse. Everything led to H. G. Higgins.

"Dad. I have a suspect."

His father drew back. "A what?"

"Someone who was at the library that day. I have his book, and I found his keys, and I know he used to live around here somewhere. It's *H. G. Higgins*, Dad. He's a famous writer, but his whole life is a secret."

"Evan—"

"We should tell the police! Or the fire warden. It's not too late, is it? And then everyone will know they were wrong about you. This is a big deal, Dad. People *died*!"

"Back up, kiddo. You're saying that you think *the writer H. G. Higgins* started the library fire?"

"Yes!"

"Why in the world do you believe that?"

"He returned a book that day—I have the book! He was there!"

"Okay. Let's say that's true. And fifty other people probably returned books that day, too."

"But his book had a picture in it—a picture someone took from the treehouse in the woods."

His dad looked at him. "Can I see it?"

Evan unzipped his bag and yanked it from the book. "That's probably him in the picture! And his keys were at the old library ground. One of them opened the padlock on the treehouse!"

His father held up the Polaroid. "This isn't H. G. Higgins. This is a terrible picture of your teacher, Mr. O'Neal. Of his eye, anyway. I took it myself when we were teenagers, with his camera."

"What?"

"Everything you're saying suggests that H. G. Higgins lived around here once. Maybe he took out that book. Maybe he climbed up to the treehouse, which, by the way, you are *not* allowed to do. But what makes you think he would set fire to the library?"

Evan didn't actually know. He just didn't want the bad guy to be anyone from Martinville. He wanted it to be someone *not from here*. "I don't know the motive, yet," he admitted. "But I'll figure it out. First we have to find him."

And that's when his father reached into his back pocket and withdrew a small envelope, folded in half. Evan caught sight of the writing and knew exactly what his dad was holding. It was the letter he had written to H. G. Higgins.

"Evan," his dad said, "I'm H. G. Higgins."

Chapter Thirty-Four

MORTIMER

Mortimer's fifth day as guardian of the library was the most momentous of all. But not until the evening.

The day had been a busy one—there had been the fifth-grade graduation, and the graduation *picnic*. So many people had visited his library! They chose books, and talked about books, and gave Mortimer several more hugs than he actually needed. Some were tighter than others.

By the time the families shook out their blankets and packed up their books, their cameras, and their desserts, Mortimer was ready to rest.

Ms. Shore, the school librarian, had carried over (one at a time) three plastic bins full of beautiful picture books. The bins did not fit under the umbrella, but they had rainproof tops, and Mortimer discovered that it was very nice to spread himself across them and gaze at the clouds.

He had heard that people thought clouds looked like sheep. That was not Mortimer's experience. He saw: a teacup, a jumping frog, a piece of cheese.

A snowball.

When he had looked at clouds for a long time, Mortimer himself felt a little like a cloud. An orange one, he supposed. A sort of *sun cloud.*

Guardian of the lib—

But he interrupted himself: *All my fault.*

Mortimer felt like a cloud that could never let go of its silver rain.

He fell asleep and dreamed of Petunia.

As soon as the sun got low, the mice began to arrive at the town green. Excited, very loud mice. They woke Mortimer up.

One small voice kept shouting about his first "grabation," and Mortimer understood that the day was a special one for more than one species in Martinville. A lot of those parent-made desserts had left big crumbs in the grass.

Mortimer lazily flipped himself over and saw that a

mouse was passing right in front of him. He didn't recognize this one. Mortimer gave him a tired wave.

The mouse stopped. "I've heard about you. You're the Six-Toed Grouch."

Mortimer lifted his head. "What?" This mouse was hard to hear, above the other mice, who were (he guessed) happily gathering cake crumbs.

"The Six-Toed Grouch!" The mouse gave a self-satisfied nod. "That's what we call you."

"Oh," said Mortimer. His heart seemed to shrink a little.

The mouse now appeared a little less satisfied with himself. "*Well?*"

"Well what?"

"Now *you're* supposed to say something."

"Okay. Something about what?"

The mouse sighed. "Stop playing games. You know, something about how I'm just a grubby little mouse, so who cares what I think?"

He walked up close to where Mortimer's chin was resting on the edge of the plastic book bin.

"*Are* you grubby?" Mortimer said.

The mouse sat down. Or sat up, depending on how you looked at it. His bottom was now planted in the grass, and his front feet were up in the air.

"That's irrelevant! And now I feel bad," he added. "I was just taking the first turn. I thought if *I* didn't, *you* would."

"What's your name?" Mortimer asked.

"Fred. Yours?"

"It's Mortimer. But everyone calls me Goldie, or Sunshine, or Buffy. Or dear cat."

"Mortimer," said Fred.

It was good to hear someone say it. Mortimer suddenly wondered how long it had been since someone had called him by his own name.

Chase me, Mortimer! Chase me!

"Is it true," Mortimer asked, "what you said? Everyone calls me the Six-Toed Grouch?"

The mouse looked down. "Yes. No. I mean, only everyone *I* know."

Even lying next to a suitcase full of poetry, Mortimer felt very much alone when he heard that.

"Look on the bright side, though. At least you aren't the Six-Toed *Monster*."

"Monster?" Mortimer lifted his head.

"Or the Gray Horror. Or the Striped Destroyer."

What were all these names supposed to mean? "Well, no. I'm orange," Mortimer said.

The mouse nodded. "Yes, I can see that."

It was time to change the subject. "Do you like poetry?" Mortimer asked.

The mouse scoffed. "I don't have time to *read.* I am a wild animal! Don't you know what that means? It means I have to find all my own food and shelter. I have to be always looking out for owls, hawks, opossums, and, you know . . ." He trailed off.

"Cats?" guessed Mortimer.

"Yes. Cats. And I must keep my brothers and sisters fed, and warm, and safe. I certainly do *not* have time to read. I shouldn't even be standing here talking to you. I should be over *there*, gathering crumbs with the others!"

Mortimer thought guiltily of his food dish, and the comfortable chair he usually shared with Ms. Scoggin by the warm fire, and Al's too-tight hugs. He thought about mouse doors one through five, and how he'd forced the mice—so many of them over the years!—to leave just as soon as they'd come in. All to protect Mr. Brock's cheese and Al's apples. The ghosts barely ate any of it. Why had he not shared?

Maybe he was much *worse* than a grouch.

Say sorry, his heart said (still feeling shrunk).

"I'm sorry," Mortimer said. The worst part, he admitted (only to himself), was that he *had* known the mice had hard lives. Of course he had known. He'd just thought it had nothing to do with him.

"Oh, well." The mouse waved at him. "I'm sorry I called you a grouch. And my life's not *so* bad. I have my family. My brothers and sisters. I'd be lost without them."

Mortimer nodded, stared glumly at his front paws, and thought about Petunia.

Following his gaze, Fred seemed to remember Mortimer's twelve front claws. "Extra toes are nice, I think. Nothing wrong with that!" He took one step backward. "I'll bet the Gray Horror wishes he had six toes on every foot!"

Something clicked. Mortimer looked sharply at Fred. "Are you saying," Mortimer said, "that the Gray Horror is real? A real cat?"

"Oh yes, very real. Lives on Elm Street. I guess you don't know him."

"And the Striped Destroyer? Also real?" Mortimer was trying not to get his hopes up.

Hope! said his heart, in a small voice.

Fred nodded. "The Striped Destroyer lives over by the train station. Good eating there, especially on holiday weekends."

Mortimer hesitated. "And, the Six-Toed Monster?" he whispered. "Real?"

"Sure. She's just like you—six on every foot. She lives in Grantville, at the movie theater, which is just *incredibly* frustrating, to be honest. We could eat for a *month* on what gets dropped at that movie theater on a single weekend, but—"

Mortimer was on his feet, his heart swelling with hope. *Hope, hope, hope!* It rushed at him from every direction.

Petunia! his heart shouted.

With great speed, Fred retreated to the other side of the poetry suitcase. "We aren't going to fight now, are we?"

"No, no!" Mortimer said. He sat down, in order to appear less . . . large. "No fighting."

Mortimer couldn't see the whole thing yet, but an idea was starting to form inside him, like clouds gathering into a shape.

He would go to Grantville. To see if Petunia was the Six-Toed Monster. But first . . . first he had to do something else.

"Can you bring your brothers and sisters?" he asked Fred. "Bring them here? I know a safe place where there are apples and potatoes. And cheese. And not just today—*every* day."

"Really?" Fred looked at him closely. "But it isn't a trick, is it? If I bring them, they'll be safe?"

"No tricks," Mortimer said. "Safe. Hurry, Fred."

Chapter Thirty-Five

MORTIMER

While he waited for Fred to come back, Mortimer looked around at his library and thought about all the people who had visited it in just these few days. He thought about Winnie D. and Mrs. Baker, and Mr. Gregorian, and Ms. Shore, and everyone else who had brought a book, or left one. He thought about faces like question marks, and the beautiful smell of books.

And the night of the fire.

Guardian of the library, he tried to tell himself.

Not quite, his heart said. Because what he was guarding was not the library.

Mortimer was guarding a secret.

* * *

Ten minutes later, Fred returned with a line of brothers and sisters in tow.

"I could only get eight," he said. "Everyone else refused to leave the picnic."

Eight brothers and sisters, Mortimer thought. *Imagine it.*

Fred introduced them: Fern, Flora, Finn (good ol' Finn!), Frank, Fiona, Faye, Fergus, and Flavia.

"All *F*s," Mortimer said, waving at Finn, who gave him a small wave back.

"Really?" Frank said. "All *F*s? I never noticed that."

Mortimer looked at him.

"He's kidding!" Flavia shouted. "Of course we've noticed!"

Mortimer scanned the brave line of them and said, "I need your help."

A few minutes later, they had a very basic plan. The mice would enter the History House through one of its five mouse doors while Mortimer got himself let in by Al through the front. They would all meet up at the fireplace in the parlor.

"Five!" Flavia shouted. "Ha! There are nine mouse holes in that old house. At *least* nine!"

"Nine?" Mortimer repeated. "Is this another joke?"

The mice assured him that it wasn't.

"Well, okay." Mortimer's confidence was slightly shaken, but there was no time to dwell on it. "Nine doors. Take your pick, I guess. When Al lets me in, I'll run straight to the parlor and jump up to the mantel. That's where we keep the matches."

"Can you even jump that high?" Flavia shouted. "You look kind of old."

"Of course I can," Mortimer said. The truth was that he planned to use Ms. Scoggin's chair to get himself up to the mantel. Once he was on the back of that chair, it was easy to hop over. But he didn't explain this to the very loud Flavia, who was beginning to remind him of Petunia.

"Where was I?" he said.

"In the parlor," Faye said.

"On the mantel," Finn added. "With the matches."

"Right. And you remember the rest of it?"

They did.

"Except you haven't told us *why*," Flavia shouted. "What's it all *for*?"

"It's for telling the truth," Mortimer told her. "And by the way, don't run away if Ms. Scoggin screams a lot right at the beginning. She's afraid of mice, but once we get started, I think she'll pay attention."

They nodded. And looked at him expectantly.

"Um. Did I forget anything?" Mortimer asked.

Fred cleared his throat. "Well. There is *one* detail, but it's not important right now, I suppose—"

"Where are the apples?" Flavia shouted. "Where is the *cheese*? And where's my *poem*? Fred said you have poems here, and I have never even *tasted* one!"

Mortimer explained.

The mice did not remember the night of the library fire. Mice, to put it bluntly, do not live that long. But they had heard about it. "We call it 'the terrible fire,'" Fred had told him. "Every mouse pup hears the story. It's why we never, ever pick up—*you* know."

"Matches," Mortimer said.

"Yes." Fred shuddered. "So you can see that we're really going the extra mile here. Breaking our rule for you, I mean."

"I am grateful," Mortimer said. "A one-time performance. We will need to be very convincing."

"We're ready," Finn said.

"Let's *go*!" Flavia shouted. She thrust a tiny fist into the air.

"Showtime!" Fred said.

"Cheese time!" Flavia shouted. "Apple time!" She gave a

little jump, landing on her back feet with her hands clasped over her head. "Potato time!"

Finn rolled his eyes. Flavia began to wobble, and Faye put out a hand to steady her.

Mortimer looked at the mice and felt . . . something.

Longing, his heart said.

And then Fred gave a practiced whistle, and everyone scattered.

Chapter Thirty-Six

AL

"Ms. Scoggin . . . ," I started carefully, setting down a new, hot cup of tea.

"Yes, dear?"

"On that night—the night of the fire, I mean."

"Yes, go on."

"Well, the fire started after closing time."

"I remember that, I suppose."

"I have sometimes wondered . . ." I hesitated again.

"My dear. You know I can't stand it when you stop talking before you have finished your own sentence!"

"Fine! Why in the world was Mr. Brock still there? It should have been just the three of us. You, me, and the boy."

Ms. Scoggin turned pink. If you have never seen a pink ghost, I can tell you that it's an interesting sight. Already hovering, she now drifted higher.

"Was Mr. Brock still there?" Ms. Scoggin said, picking some imaginary lint off her shoulder and suddenly trying to act bored.

"Of course he was still there, Ms. Scoggin! Otherwise he would not have been trapped and—"

"Yes, you are right, of course," Ms. Scoggin interrupted. Now she was impatient. She landed gently in her chair. "If you must know, he was waiting for me to finish up my work. We had plans that evening."

"Plans? Do you mean a date, Ms. Scoggin?"

Ms. Scoggin nodded, once. "We were going to the movies in Grantville that night. Or, we *thought* we were."

We heard a soft sigh.

Mr. Brock had been sitting on the small sofa all this time. Since he never acknowledged me, I had long before stopped worrying about what I said in front of him. But now he surprised us both by lowering his book to his lap and speaking loudly. "The movies! Yes. We never *did* get to see that movie, did we? I *do* hope there will be movies where we are going next, Ms. Scoggin. Have I mentioned? That is one of the things I am *most* looking forward to."

"Next?" I said.

Ms. Scoggin tried to shush him.

"I am *most* looking forward to movies," he repeated. "*Quite* soon," he added, picking up his book. It slipped through his fingers once, but he made another grab and managed to hold it up to his face.

I put my hands on my hips. "Ms. Scoggin, where are we going?"

Before she had a chance to answer me, Mr. Brock, still holding his book, began to rise. First, he was only a foot or so above the parlor sofa, apparently still reading. But very soon, he rose higher. Then his head was halfway through the ceiling.

"Ms. Scoggin!" he called. His book fell to the floor. "Ms. Scoggin!"

"Mr. Brock!" For some reason, Ms. Scoggin seized my wrist. With her other hand, she reached up for Mr. Brock's ankle. He stopped going up, but did not come down either, and we held together like that. Awkwardly.

And then, mice began to flood the room.

Mice. From a few different directions. I counted at least six of them.

"Agh! *Agh!*" Ms. Scoggin said. But she did not let go of either of us.

She did, however, begin to rise up from the floor again, pulling me with her until I was stretched, and on tippy toes.

Mr. Brock was mostly through the ceiling now, Ms. Scoggin hanging from his ankle, and me from her. I gripped her forearm and she gripped mine.

In order to anchor us, I grabbed the mantelpiece with my free hand.

Mr. Brock's voice came faintly but clearly from the other side of the ceiling. "Ms. Scoggin! We must go, if we are going, I believe!"

She looked at me. "My dear," she said. "Can I do anything else for you?"

I wondered what on Earth was she talking about. "I've got the mantelpiece!" I cried. "Don't worry, whatever happens, I will not let go!"

She looked back at me. I felt her fingers slip a bit on my arm, but she squeezed harder, and held me.

"You are on your way, my dear. Your small library is a success. And today you have met a brand-new patron."

"Patron?" I repeated.

"You know your place again," she said. "At last."

"Our place is here, Ms. Scoggin! Our perfect house!"

Her head was almost at the ceiling now, and mine was

hanging sideways, one arm reaching up to her, one clinging to the thin marble edge of the mantelpiece.

"My dear," she said gently.

I looked back at her and said nothing.

"If you let go," she said, "I will let go."

"What do you mean?" I yelled. "I am the one holding us down!"

"Exactly," she said.

The six (or now possibly eight?) mice had gathered on the hearth just below us. I watched them, and squeezed the mantelpiece, and pretended not to understand her.

I could not hear Mr. Brock anymore, but Ms. Scoggin still held his ankle. Her grip on me slipped again, but we quickly caught each other by the fingers. And squeezed. Anchored by the mantel, we were more or less stationary. An odd kite, waving slightly. I looked up at the sole of Mr. Brock's shoe.

"If you can let go, I can let go," she repeated. Strangely, she sounded more patient than I had ever known her to be in life (or death).

Mr. Brock was not coming back down. That much was obvious.

I considered. She was asking a lot. But she was, after all, my supervisor.

"All right," I said finally.

She nodded. "I love you, my dear."

I loved her, too. I let go of the mantelpiece.

In the same instant, she let go of me. I fell heavily to the rug, where several mice came to investigate me. Ms. Scoggin hovered for a moment, and then began to rise.

I watched Mr. Brock's foot, and then my beloved Ms. Scoggin, disappear through the ceiling. And I heard two final words, summoned by Mr. Brock.

"What courage!"

I believe he was talking about me.

Chapter Thirty-Seven
EVAN

HOW Evan felt that night:

1. confused.
2. very confused.

When the mosquitoes came out, he and his father abandoned the rock of truth, which Evan didn't mind one bit. He'd had enough truth for one day. They moved into the kitchen, where his mom had left them some soup, along with a note explaining that she'd gone on a house call to restart someone's router.

Evan's father was H. G. Higgins. The famous writer.

His dad had explained: He made up the name when he

was a teenager. He *had* taken out *How to Write a Mystery Novel*, and read it. And he'd started writing. He'd done it: Gotten published. Gotten *famous*.

"Why don't you want anyone to know?" Evan asked.

"A few people know. Jonathan O'Neal, for one. He's the one who gave me your letter."

Oh. That was what Evan had seen after the bus trip to Grantville. Mr. O'Neal had handed over Evan's letter. *That* was the "paperwork."

"But mostly I just like to be private, I guess. I like my little office in the cellar. I like being here, with you guys, in the house where I grew up. I don't want book tours and interviews and all that."

"Does this mean we're rich?"

His dad smiled. "We have some money."

"But what about the mice?"

"What about them?"

"I mean—what's the mystery there?"

His dad shrugged. "All country towns have mice. I keep driving them over the hill and hoping they stay put so that some other guy doesn't kill them."

"But *why*? Why are you trying to save them?"

"No big mystery. I have a soft spot for mice. Since I was a kid."

They were both quiet for a minute. And then Evan said, "How rich are we, exactly?"

The soup, on top of the whole long day, made Evan sleepy, though it was officially too early for sleep. He dropped into bed anyway, still wearing his button-down graduation shirt. His mind was bouncing. He'd been *right*. H. G. Higgins *had* lived in Martinville. But Evan still had no idea who set the library on fire.

After a few minutes, he sat up, found the mystery keys in his backpack, and ran back downstairs in his socks. He needed to check something.

From the kitchen, he could hear his dad typing away, as usual, in the cellar. *Oh.* Maybe it had been silly to believe that an exterminator had that many emails to answer. But who really thought about the actual *things* their parents did for work?

Evan left the house quietly through the kitchen door and tried not to crunch too loudly on the gravel—*ouch, no shoes*—as he walked past his father's cellar-office window and around to the front of the house.

He fit the second key, the bigger one, into their front door and turned the knob. The door swung open. He stepped inside and closed it behind him. One more fact, confirmed: These had been his dad's keys, a long time ago.

Evan leaned against the door and listened to the faint sound of his father's keyboard-tapping. He closed his eyes and imagined his dad, just a kid, walking to the library with these keys in his front pocket.

That's when he remembered the book.

The *other* book.

Back in his room, Evan got down on the rug and felt around under his bed until his fingers found it: the falling-apart book with the taped-up cover.

He looked at the dates on the circulation card and did the math in his head. His father had read this book at least twice a year, every year, starting the summer he was eight, until the year the library burned down.

Without even getting up from the floor, Evan opened his father's library book and started to read it.

It was about a mouse.

And suddenly, Evan understood. His father's "soft spot" for mice had started right here, with the book in his hands. Everything went back to the library.

His dad deserved justice. His dad deserved to be able

to talk to people in town without feeling like they were suspicious of him.

Evan had been pretty good at this detective thing so far. What were the chances of finding a set of keys his *own father* had dropped twenty years ago? Not even Mr. O'Neal could find an equation for that.

Evan pictured the keys waiting in the dirt in the middle of all those thorny weeds. He thought of the cat, standing above them. Not budging until Evan picked them up.

Did the *cat* know something? He couldn't exactly ask him. But maybe he could ask his owner.

Evan sat up, not tired anymore. He put down the book.

And reached for his sneakers.

Chapter Thirty-Eight
AL

So here's the truth of it, the truth Ms. Scoggin finally made me face: I'm not a ghost. I was never a ghost.

In fact, I am like anyone who is alive.

I did not die on the night of the fire, though I came close. I remember collapsing in the library basement, my lungs full of smoke.

I had shoved the cart (and the dear cat) through the basement door and then, by crawling, found Edward, finally, on the floor. He looked unconscious, and I grabbed at his arms, preparing to drag him out. Instead, without meaning to, I joined him on the ground.

And then, somehow, Edward got me outside.

Saved me.

I woke up on sharp gravel in the cold night air. Edward was next to me, coughing and coughing. There were sirens, and a firefighter was running toward us.

"Is anyone inside?" he shouted.

And I told him, *Ms. Scoggin*. Ms. Scoggin!

They found her on the balcony, where she had been overcome by smoke.

After that—how can I explain? I suppose my heart broke.

I felt myself draining away. I *wanted* to become a ghost.

And then, somehow, a miracle, she was next to me. My dear Ms. Scoggin. A ghost, but also, herself.

We moved into the History House together, along with Mr. Brock.

I made the applesauce, and baked the potatoes, and managed the cheese cupboard. I am ashamed to say that it never even occurred to me that the dear ghosts wished to be someplace else.

Instead, Ms. Scoggin stayed and stayed. For *me*.

She waited for me to take my place in the world again. Waited for me to let go of her.

This, I believe, is similar to what mothers do.

I never thanked her.

I never thanked Mr. Brock, who waited with her. (And twenty years is a very long time to wait for a trip to the movies.)

I never even thanked Edward for saving my life.

Instead, I hid. I did my Monday errands with my head down. And if anyone spoke to me, I rushed in the other direction. But most people learned not to talk to me. No one tried anymore, after a while. Not even the person who made me those tuna fish and pickle sandwiches every Wednesday.

After the dear ghosts left, I lay on the parlor floor with a big bump on my head, contemplating all of this.

And then, for the second time in one day, I heard a knock at the door.

Chapter Thirty-Nine
MORTIMER

Mortimer had waited on the History House porch while the mice chose their preferred doors and quickly disappeared inside.

When enough time had passed for them to have gathered in the parlor, Mortimer scratched at the front door. And waited.

He scratched again. And yelled, “It’s me!”

And waited.

Where in the world was Al? The mice would be wondering where he was. He scratched the door one more time.

Suddenly, a tiny body popped onto the porch from the crack under the door (also known as mouse door number one).

"What's taking so long?" Flavia demanded. "We are all by the fireplace, waiting for you to spill the matches!"

"I can't get in," Mortimer said. "I need Al to open up."

"Who is *Al*? Is she the lady on the floor?"

Mortimer stared at her. "What do you mean, on the floor?"

"I mean *on the floor*." Flavia flopped down to demonstrate.

"Maybe one of the ghosts can manage to let me in," he said.

Still flat on her back, Flavia shook her head. "No ghosts in there."

"No ghosts? Are you *sure*?"

"Oh yes. My hearing is excellent. Better than yours. In fact, my hearing is right now telling me that there is a human just around the corner." And then she sat up and scuttled back under the door. "Maybe ask the human!" she shouted from the other side. "And hurry up!"

Mortimer realized that she was right. Someone was coming down the path behind him, and then, loudly, up the porch steps.

It was Evan. The boy with the question-mark face. Mortimer looked up at him and tapped his paw repeatedly on the front door, hinting.

"Goldie!" Evan said, shining his flashlight right at him.

"You must be locked out." He knocked on the door, three times.

From inside, they heard one word. "Help!"

They looked at each other. Evan tried the doorknob. Locked.

"Should I break the glass?" Evan said.

Mortimer wanted to tell him that there was a key under the mat.

"Don't break the glass," someone called out from behind them. "There's probably a key under the doormat."

Evan whirled around. "*Dad?*"

Mortimer realized that this "someone" was none other than the town exterminator, who drove around in a van that said "Mission Mouse." What were these two doing here?

The ghosts were gone?

Al was on the floor?

Unexpected visitors?

This was the problem with plans, Mortimer thought. They often went sideways. He wasn't sure how much patience an exterminator would have for the mice's performance. They would have to get their point across very quickly, he decided. At least Al was inside. That was good. She was the one who mattered. He hoped she would get up from the floor.

Evan and his father had found the key that was indeed under the mat. They were opening the door.

Mortimer stretched his long body. He was ready. He would get to those matches before anything else could go wrong.

Chapter Forty

EVERYONE

"Are you . . . seeing this?" Evan's father asked.

"I *think* so," the cheese lady said, rubbing her temple slowly, as if she might have a headache.

Evan could only stare. The mice were doing a dance or something.

It was impossible. But also, it was happening.

They were marching around in a little circle now, holding *matchsticks* in their mouths.

And the cat appeared to be—supervising?

If anyone deserved a secret mouse dance, Evan thought, it was his father.

"Unless I hit my head a little harder than I thought I

did," the cheese lady said. She was still wearing the pin that said "AL."

Al saved me, his father had said. It was why Evan had come back here.

Al.

AL.

If this was the "Al" his dad talked about, maybe she would know what really happened on the night of the fire. Evan had come to ask her.

But he was obviously going to have to wait.

Am I hallucinating? Al wondered.

Edward (the dear boy! But no longer a boy, of course) had helped her up from the floor, and now the mice appeared to be putting on some kind of *play*. She didn't know which thing was more impossible.

It *felt* like a play, anyway. The dear cat had jumped to the mantel, knocked over the heavy matchstick cup with one of his giant paws, and was now standing tall on the hearthstone.

The mice dived for the matchsticks as soon as they hit the ground, and then stood between the dear cat's large front feet.

Nine mice, in a neat line. Each of them holding a matchstick firmly in its mouth.

And then, at an invisible sign (it was actually just another whistle from Fred, but the humans couldn't hear it), the mice began to parade in a circle around the dear cat.

Slowly, the cat raised a six-toed paw above his head—it seemed for a moment that he was about to strike. Instead, he gave the air above the mice a vague swipe. The dear cat was *acting*.

At this, the mice *acted* afraid—they zigzagged around in front of the fireplace, dipping their heads so that their matches sparked against the hearthstone.

Matches.

Al heard a sharp inhale, and realized she had made the noise herself.

Edward stood like a stone beside her.

Then the mice stopped their zigzagging and match-sparking, and lined up neatly again in front of Mortimer. They dropped their matches—all but the smallest mouse, who raced over to where Mr. Brock's book was still facedown on the floor and stood on top of it, balancing on her two hind legs with her match in her mouth.

What a dear mouse, Al thought. (But Ms. Scoggin

would be *horrified*—a book spread out on its face! With a *mouse* standing on top of it!)

Of course, Ms. Scoggin was gone. That knowledge was still sinking in. The more Al absorbed it, the more she was sure she would cry.

Concentrate, she told herself.

The dear cat had begun to meow. A lot.

In fact, Mortimer was speaking. Here is what he said:

My sister Petunia and I chased a poor mouse that night in the library.

We didn't know it had a matchstick in its mouth.

We were just kittens.

Then everything was on fire, and we ran in different directions.

The fire was my fault.

And also an accident.

I am deeply sorry about it.

I never saw Petunia again.

The mice say she may be a monster in Grantville who likes movies, and I am going to find out for myself.

One more thing.

I told the mice they could stay here for a while.

They enjoy apples and cheese.

And probably potatoes.

Goodbye. And thanks for all the hugs.

Mortimer had wanted to write a beautiful goodbye poem to go with his speech. But there had been no time.

He knew that humans couldn't understand him. But he needed to say the words out loud anyway: "It was an accident. I'm sorry."

So sorry, his heart said.

"Nice speech!" Flavia shouted at him. "Now point me at the apples!"

"*Please*," Fred reminded her.

"Apples, please!" said Flavia.

It is true that Al, Edward, and Evan didn't understand a word Mortimer said. But they understood the performance.

Not every story needs words.

The humans turned to each other. "Mice!" Al said.

Edward nodded. He didn't look like a stone anymore. "Mice," he said.

And for the first time in many years, they were able to look at each other.

"I never even thanked you," Al said.

"Thanked *me*?" Edward said. "What for?"

"For saving my life on the night of the fire—I don't know how you did it. I found you curled up on the floor. You looked unconscious, to be honest. But then somehow you got me out."

Edward shook his head. "I didn't save *your* life, you saved *mine*! All I remember is collapsing on the floor and then waking up outside in the parking lot with you next to me. *You* must have dragged *me* out."

At that moment, something fell from the ceiling and hit the ground between their feet.

Al bent down to pick it up. It was a small plastic pin that read "Librarian."

She looked at Edward. She looked at the ceiling.

And then she cried a little.

By this time, the mice had already scattered to the basement and discovered the potato bin.

When Mortimer walked out the door, no one even noticed.

Except for Flavia.

"Bye, Mortimer!" she yelled from behind mouse door

number four. "Goodbye and good luck! I mostly don't think you're a grouch anymore!"

On the road home, Evan said, "Dad, did those mice and that cat really just show us how the fire started?"

His father nodded. "I think they did. I'm still processing it."

Evan shined the flashlight so they wouldn't trip. "We have to tell the fire warden. He can reopen the case. Right?"

Slowly, his dad nodded again. "I think we can ask him to look into it. But we probably shouldn't, um, tell him about the cat-and-mouse play. That was just for us, I think. And for Al."

Evan agreed. He would tell Rafe, though. And Mom, of course.

They had reached their house. Evan had just one more question.

"Dad? Are we the kind of rich that could build a new library?"

MORTIMER'S EPILOGUE

At the ten o'clock movie

Mortimer sat next to Petunia, tired but happy. The walk to Grantville had been a long one for an old cat.

They were in the projector room, behind a large square window, ready to watch the movie. Below them, the audience sat in plush red velvet chairs, eating popcorn.

Every once in a while, Petunia would tap him on the ear with her paw and whisper, "Mortimer! Is it really you?"

And, each time, Mortimer said, "Petunia, it's really me."

His heart was full and happy. And quiet.

The popcorn smelled so good. Mortimer understood why the mice wished they could have some. He planned to talk to Petunia about that.

The lights dimmed.

"It's starting!" Petunia whispered.

Mortimer noticed two figures hurrying to seat themselves in the first row of plush red chairs. One of them carried a box of popcorn.

They held hands through the whole movie and didn't get up when it ended. They seemed ready to watch it all over again.

As Mortimer watched, one of the figures appeared to float out of her chair, just a little, and then quickly settle down again.

Could it be? Mortimer decided to observe them more closely.

But Petunia was finished with sitting still.

"Chase me, Mortimer!" she called out. "Chase me!"

And Mortimer did.

EVAN'S EPILOGUE

On the first day of middle school

It turned out that Evan's house was the very first stop for the school bus, so he ended up saving a seat for Demetri, instead of the other way around. When Rafe got on, carrying a large paper bag, they squeezed in to make room for him.

"Tomato?" Rafe pointed at the bag in his lap.

Demetri laughed. "Maybe later."

"Sure thing." Rafe patted his bag. "Anytime. I thought I'd hand these out to my teachers today. You know, like apples?"

"Except—tomatoes," Evan said.

"Exactly." Over the summer, Rafe had proven to be a natural gardener, although he said he owed his success to the book he'd found at the little free library.

Evan looked at his watch. There would be no getting to school early this year. He itched to open his journal. He'd been writing a lot lately.

When the bus turned the corner at the town green, the library construction came into full view. So far, it was just a massive hole.

Their bus slowed to a stop at the red light. Evan had been on several site visits with his dad. Next to the massive hole, there was the now-familiar sign with a drawing of what the library was going to look like when it was finished.

It was going to look very impressive.

Demetri pointed at a small group of people standing together in hard hats, near the sign. "Isn't that your dad, Evan?"

"Yeah," Evan said. "He's been spending a lot of time there. Planning."

"Is it true they're going to call it the H. G. Higgins Library?"

"No way," Evan said. "That's just a rumor. My dad would never want it named after him." But Evan wasn't looking at the construction site anymore. He was looking at the History House.

Demetri shrugged. "Why not? He's paying for it, isn't he? I read *Assignment Accepted* over the summer, as soon as I found out about him being H. G. Higgins. And it was so good! Where did your dad learn to write? Where does he get the ideas from?"

"Right here, I guess," Evan said. "He's always lived here." The History House door opened, and Al stepped out, carrying a big tote bag over her shoulder. Evan could see a few books sticking out of it.

Demetri said. "I always thought writers were from someplace special, you know?"

Al stepped down from her porch and crossed in front of them on her way to the town green, waving cheerily at the bus driver. At the little free library, she stopped, took the bag from her shoulder, and began to shelve her books. The library had a bench now, with a jar of dog treats stowed beneath it. The beautiful orange cat hadn't returned, but someone had painted a pretty good portrait of him on the side of the library. As Evan watched, Al blew the cat a kiss before setting off again.

The light changed, and the bus lurched forward.

“Maybe *this* is someplace special,” Evan said. “Maybe everywhere is special to the people who live there.”

“Yeah,” Rafe said, biting into a tomato. “Maybe.”

The fire warden had agreed to reopen the investigation of the library fire, because he had never considered the possible role of mice. It turned out that it wasn’t all that unusual for a mouse to start a fire. Sometimes they nibbled wires. Rarely (but sometimes), they ran with matches in their mouths. Matches that dragged on things like walls, or books, and burst into flame. After a month of review, the warden officially announced that the library fire had been started by accident: “the result of unanticipated animal behavior or interference.”

Justice had been done in the end.

And this, in fact, is the end.

Almost.

AL'S EPILOGUE

One year later

The new Martinville Library stood on the footprint of the old one, but that was all that the two buildings had in common.

The new library had glass walls, five floors of books, nine cozy reading nooks, an automatic returned-books sorting machine, an elevator, a movie theater that doubled as a performance stage, three computer and virtual-reality rooms, a café, a book club meeting area, and an entire room dedicated to graphic novels and comic books.

From her glass-walled office on the third floor, the librarian could see most of what was happening in her library at any given moment. Not that she had many free moments. People—staff, patrons, friends—were always knocking on her office door, despite the large sign she had taped up: DON'T BOTHER KNOCKING—JUST COME IN!

Her intern, however, usually just stuck his head in. "Hi. You ready?"

Al looked up from her computer, where she had been making notes for the summer reading festival. "Rafe!" she said. "Oh my gosh—is school over already?" She put down the tuna and dill pickle sandwich she'd been eating. (Edward, who had admitted that he'd left those sandwiches on her porch all those years, still insisted on making one for her every Wednesday.)

Rafe grinned at her. Al was sort of famous for losing track of time. "It's almost four o'clock," he said.

"Oh!" She began to close all the documents on her screen, saving each one first. It had taken her a while to get the hang of "computer things," but dear Edward's wife, Martina, had been extremely patient with her. They'd become good friends in the past year. (Martina, who was in charge of all the tech rooms in the library, especially enjoyed Al's odd habit of handing her a cup of tea and a slice of cheese most afternoons around four o'clock.)

Al stood up, adjusted her librarian pin, and picked up the neat stack of books that had been sitting on her desk beside a small carved wood mouse. She touched the mouse for luck, or maybe just out of affection, and looked expectantly at her intern.

"I've got everything set up," Rafe said. "Extra floor cushions, like you said."

"Thank you, Rafe." Al glanced out the window to the green, where she saw a number of kids drifting from the elementary school toward the library, some of them talking and laughing, and others just thinking their private thoughts.

"I'm ready," she said.

It was time for Wednesday Book Club.

THE ONLY THING YOU ABSOLUTELY HAVE TO KNOW IS THE LOCATION OF THE LIBRARY.

—Albert Einstein

Thank you for reading this Feiwel & Friends book.
The friends who made THE LOST LIBRARY possible are:

JEAN FEIWEL, Publisher
LIZ SZABLA, VP, Associate Publisher
RICH DEAS, Senior Creative Director
HOLLY WEST, Senior Editor
ANNA ROBERTO, Senior Editor
KAT BRZOZOWSKI, Senior Editor
DAWN RYAN, Executive Managing Editor
KIM WAYMER, Senior Production Manager
EMILY SETTLE, Editor
RACHEL DIEBEL, Editor
FOYINSI ADEGBONMIRE, Associate Editor
BRITTANY GROVES, Assistant Editor
L. WHITT, Designer
HELEN SEACHRIST, Senior Production Editor